Til Love Do Us Start

A. J. DAILEY

Martin and Bowman
1-855-921-1348

CHAPTER 1

*I*t was a cold, dreary, wintry day. No snow had fallen this year, but things were destined to change tonight, according to the weather forecast. John Stevens was not in a mood to really care at all what might happen in this city. He was in a taxi, on his way to catch a ride on an airplane. He was going on a one-way journey to a new life. On the way to an unknown future.

He was leaving almost nothing but memories. Hardly any family, a used-to-be girlfriend, an elderly grandmother, but an awful lot of remembrances he would always have with him. Every street the cab crossed held some of those memories, as this town was where he was born and raised.

They passed Third street, the location of his first job. A paper route that included this area. His dad had insisted he develope a good work ethic as he grew into a young man. A pang of utter despair would have brought him to his knees, if he had been standing, by the recall of his father. His memory, coupled with their coming up on Main street, triggered the reaction.

It was on this road, just ten days ago, that he rode in a funeral procession, following a hearse carrying his father, his mother, and his teenage baby sister; all killed in an automobile accident. There was so much pain he felt for the loss of his parents. He loved them dearly, but the death of Jeanie was the crusher. She was four years younger, but they had a very close relationship as brother and sister.

CHAPTER 2

John recalled the night Jeanie came home from a date, sobbing, with a torn dress. 'Jack tried to force himself on me', she told her father.

The man's first reaction was to call the police. John had put his arms around the girl, to console her.

'Dad, let me handle this', he said. 'I'll make him wish, with all his heart, he had never touched my sister', he said.

'What are planning on?', his father asked.

'I won't touch him, unless he provokes me, Dad. I know of this guy, and he will not have another peaceful day in our school. He will be the target of every athlete there. He will be badly abused, believe me, mostly through intimidation. The prospect of facing my friends every day will be punishment, for sure' he said.

'I don't want revenge, John. I'm not hurt physically, just upset he would do this to me', she said.

'Jeanie, this guy knows you are my sister, so what he did was challenge to us both. It must be dealt with, without resorting to violence, unless he wants it', John said.

The fact his son was the star football player at the school was assurance to Mr. Stevens the matter concerning his daughter would be dealt with.

CHAPTER 3

*T*he Stevens were a close-knit family. A father who was a successful businessman. A stay-at-home mother, who home-schooled her children all the way to high school. When they entered public school, they excelled in academics and sports. They knew most of the kids in town through church and social events and it was an easy move for them. Mom made sure they had an open house for parties and get togethers for their friends. It was a must among the town folks to be a part of their group. Now, except for dad's mother, Grandma Stevens, and himself, the whole family was gone.

CHAPTER 4

Over on the other side of town, another family story was unfolding. A young beautiful teenager had also experienced a traumatic event. It was a complete game-changer for the girl, and would lead to events that could only be described as — magical!

Suzie could not imagine the change that had affected her life in the last year, or so. She was starting her senior semester in high school. She advanced her graduation a half year by taking extra classes, and would be through in a couple months, at mid-term.

Everything was planned for her future, except the sudden and unexpected death of her father. Her very first memories were almost all about him. She was an only child, pretty and smart. And she loved her daddy! He doted over the child, and the two were very close. His death seemed to be the end of her world, except they both were devout Christians. Suzie's father started taking her to church with him from the beginning. She could not remember missing a Sunday sitting in a pew and watching her dad singing in the choir. One of her dreams was to grow up and join him there. 'I will see you again, Pappa', she said as she leaned over and kissed him goodbye.

CHAPTER 5

$\mathcal{J}$ ohn had a bunch of close friends from high school, college, and law school. They all were as shocked as he was by the sudden and tragic death of his family and their wonderful support made the hours and days bearable. He had gotten his degree only a few months earlier. He passed the bar exams, and got his license to practice as an attorney. Professor Hamilton, the head of the law school, had sort of adopted him, since he had no children, and John had excelled as a student.

'I feel so empty, Professor. Dad and mom and Jeanie were so much a part of my life. I can't seem to shake the depression I'm in', he said.

Mr. Hamilton spoke up.

'I can only imagine your hurt, John. They were always there for you. But they taught you well, and their love is what will bring you through this crisis. What you need is a change venue. I have recommended you to a law firm up north. They have your vital statistics, and they want you to visit them', the professor said.

John had not considered leaving town, even after the accident. He had thought he would continue his father's business, but he never felt much of an urge to do so.

The chance to get to work, and at the same time giving him some space from everything, suddenly felt attractive.

'Okay, it will take a couple weeks to clean things up here. You know Joe Greene, Professor. He was dad's attorney. I hired him to handle selling the company', John stated.

'Yes, I know him. I'll keep in touch with him', Professor Hamilton answered.

CHAPTER 6

Suzie's personality was, to a large degree, shaped by her father and her church. She finally became old enough to join her dad in the choir. He had insisted she have proper voice training and she developed a beautiful soprano voice. This led to an even closer relationship between father and daughter. Her mother showed no interest in their music, and very little desire to join them in church affairs. She was happy in her circle of activities that did not include Suzie.

The death of her father left the young teenager with little support from her mother, and she wavered in her commitments to the church. She was still completely devoted to her faith in her Savior, but she dropped out of the choir. Her thoughts were that she must have time to get past this overwhelming sense of dispair.

The one event that added to this turmoil in her life, was her mother's reaction to her losing her husband. She spent some time in mourning, but not nearly as long as Suzie expected her to do.

'Life must go on', she said. 'Your father is gone and you are no help to me. He spent more time with you than with me, anyway', she said. 'I am going to resume living, Suzie. I have met a man and will start seeing him. We are interested in each other, and I will marry him if he proposes', she said.

Two months later they were married, and Bill Sloan moved in.

CHAPTER 7

Suzie put off starting college. She had planned on attending the local university, but instead, she began volunteer work at the church's day-care facility. She loved helping with the babies. This was something she truly enjoyed.

Susan loved helping with their care, and it kept her away from his stepfather. She made no effort to interact with him in any way. There was no rudeness on her part. Just a total lack of desire of wanting to talk to him. she was polite, but avoided all his attempts to talk to her, as it made her very nervous being around him.

Susan decided to go to a school out-of-state, instead of to the local university, as was her original plans. The church work would keep her busy, until then, she thought. Little did she know those plans would change, in a big way.

CHAPTER 8

John decided he would keep the family house. All his life's memories were in that beautiful place, but it could not stay unoccupied. 'Grandma Stevens', he thought. She lived in a retirement home a short distance away, since the death of Grandpa.

He drove the next day to see her. 'Oh, John, I'm so glad you came by. Even though you have called every day, the loneliness is almost overwhelming', she said.

He knew she wasn't doing well since the funeral. Jeanie was her favorite. They had talked every day, sharing confidences only female relatives can do.

'Grandma, I have been offered a position up north. I would like for you to take over our house. I will provide around the clock care for you. I know so many things around there will be painful reminders, but it would be a big help to me', he said.

'Oh, John. There is nowhere on this earth I would rather live. Your dad wanted me to live with them after Grandpa's death, but I felt it would burden them. All of you were so good at calling and visiting, and I was glad I made that decision. Now, I will be so glad to be close to my friends, and I can visit Grandpa. I'll spend a lot of time there, John, and the others will seem closer to me, also', she said.

His dad had left all the affairs of both the company and the family in good order, so he was able to breeze through them in short order. Which left only his girlfriend to deal with. It was not a serious matter on his part as he had refused to allow things to go beyond casual dates. Beth wanted more and it all hit the fan last night. John would not go further than hugs and kisses, but the beautiful young lady demanded more. She wanted to comfort him in his grief by having sex.

'I love you, John', she said. 'Let me show you how much', she said.

'Beth, you know how I feel about the matter of intimacy. I want to save myself for my bride', he said. 'Well, let's go then, I want to be your wife', she whispered.

'Right now, all I can think of is my dead family. I will discuss this with you tomorrow', he answered.

CHAPTER 9

*A*s they crossed the bridge entering the airport, he recalled the phone call he made to Beth a couple of days later. He intentionally delayed the conversation, hoping the girl would get annoyed and end the relationship herself. She was a real beauty and John felt it was important for her to be the one ending everything.

'John, I have decided to take a step backward, so to speak. You have been through an awful lot, so let's give it a rest right for the time being', she said.

'Thanks, Beth. You have eased my burden. I have been offered a position out of town, and I'll be leaving tomorrow. We'll see how matters shape up between us', he said.

Beth could not believe how this whole business was playing out. She had never felt this way about a man. He was handsome, a famous football star, and a lawyer. What a catch, she thought. Yet, here he was, saying goodbye, and there was nothing she could do to stop him. 'Oh, well. I guess my future is with old faithful-George', she sighed.

CHAPTER 10

*F*rom the other side of town, another cab was headed for the airport. Suzie had a plane to catch. She was alone, and also on a one-way journey, probably never to return to her hometown.

The driver kept glancing in his mirror at the extremely attractive fare. He could not remember having such a young girl riding alone to the airport. He noticed a down-cast look on her face, and wondered what the heck was going on in her life.

Suzie boarded the plane and found her assigned seat. She was alone toward the back of the plane, which was fine with her. She did not feel like socializing today.

John's cab was at the airport. and not any too soon. He would have to hurry it up. He was almost late, he thought. But as it is in most cases, the plane was delayed a few minutes, so no worry, he made it alright. As he walked down the aisle, he noted the plane was a long way from being filled.

Since he was one of the last passengers to board, he guessed the plane was about one-third full. He found his assigned seat, and could see a pretty young lady was in the window seat of his row. They were only a few rows in front of the wall of the mid-plane galley.

They were on a jet with twin engines mounted in front of the tail section. He could not see the section behind the galley, but he assumed they were the only ones in the rear of the plane. He nodded in recognition to the girl, and her response had been a weak smile.

There seemed to be a sadness behind her beautiful hazel eyes. Too much for a girl her age, which he guessed at 16 or 17 years old. He had noted that she had followed his approach toward his seat. This had truly raised his spirits, though he knew she was a teenager, but her beauty and subdued demeanor were very appealing.

CHAPTER 11

Suzie's attention had been drawn to the young man coming down the aisle toward her. She had a vague feeling he was familiar. There was no way she would have forgotten ever meeting such a handsome man without remembering it. She was very pleased when he stopped at her row and proceeded to occupy the aisle seat.

Although he was somewhat accustomed to female attention, it was nice when it happened. He was taller than average height. Coupled with an easy athletic gait and good looks, it gave him an air of confidence. He had recently turned 21, although he looked younger. Many times in the past, people had mentioned the fact. When they found out he was a full -fledged attorney, which meant he was a college graduate, several expressed doubt. His response was always just a smile. A former classmate once told him that he came across as somewhat smug. That comment affected him a lot. From then on, he merely nodded.

CHAPTER 12

*W*inter had just started and he reckoned that was the reason for the low number of passengers headed north. He was glad the plane was not full, as he needed to work on his resume, and would need the extra room. He was prepared to move to another row of seats after take-off.

As he settled in, he looked toward the window, and he and the young lady's eyes met. He was struck by her beauty, and it gave him a strange feeling that he could not identify. His admiration must have shown in his face. A faint smile on her countenance made it clear she was no stranger to male attention. Yet, the sadness was evident.

'It looks like we will be taking off into some very active weather', John said, as he noted the dark clouds in the sky. She had put a pillow in her lap, and John surmised she was prepared to take a nap as soon as they were air-borne. 'I will move to another row and give you room to stretch, just as soon as I can', he said.

'Don't leave, please. This is my first plane ride, and it has made me a little nervous. I was hoping for some companionship', she said.

John was surprised by her request. As he sat looking at her, he was still pondering his uneasiness. He wondered, was it because she was alone on a plane headed north, at this time of the year. Or maybe he was thinking she should be in school. But it made him feel good hearing her personal remark. He felt an urge to become acquainted with this female. He was certain she was too young for him to have any romantic interest in her. There was no thought of trying to impress her, but something about this young lady was really bugging him. He was never a person to go from highs to lows so quickly, especially since the accident.

And this was what is happening now, he thought. He told himself to relax. All these changes to his lifestyle were probably the reasons for his tension. He would settle back and enjoy the presence of this very pretty female. Maybe they both had some matter in their lives that needed time and distance to forget.

CHAPTER 13

*T*he plane began its take-off, and the noise of the engines stopped any thought of conversation. John waited until the seat belt sign went off, and turned to face the young lady. 'I'm John Stevens', he said as he extended his hand.

'My name is Suzie Wells', and as she took his hand, their eyes met again. And she smiled up at him.

This time, it was a good one, not forced or weak. 'Thank you for the invite to talk, Suzie', he said. 'I have had some bad luck this past several weeks'.

He was about to mention the accident, and had turned toward Suzie, just as she did the same. For the first time, they were face to face. Suddenly, he realized what had bothered him before. Suzie looked so much like his little sister.

Now, he understood his attraction to this woman. Not in a sexual way, but the same way he felt toward Jeanie. Tears welled up in his eyes, and Suzie's face showed what she was thinking. What is going on here, she thought.

CHAPTER 14

*J*ohn composed himself, and made no mention of why the surprise emotions. He didn't think it would be wise to explain himself, truthfully, at this time. He decided to contribute the reaction to the accident. 'I lost my father, mother, and baby sister in a car accident a couple weeks ago', he said. 'My sister Jeanie was about your age, beautiful as you are, and resembles you a whole lot. Seeing someone like you really floored me. I'll never get over her death, and I thought I had her loss under control. I know now I do not. I'm sorry', he said.

CHAPTER 15

*S*uzie was overwhelmed, as she listened to this young man tell his story, the grief showing in his face. She wanted to put her arms around him and hug the pain away. It was a fleeting thought, as she realized that would not be a fitting move on her part. Instead, she just looked at him, but sensing a new emotion she had never felt before.

Then she realized why she thought the young man looked familiar. 'I remember seeing your story on the television. You were at the cemetery with your grandmother, and my thought was how sad you both looked', she said.

She was trying to sort this out in her mind, when the seat belt sign came on. 'Please buckle your seat belt. Rough weather coming up', said the captain. Both John and Suzie were relieved by the distraction, as the tension eased. They sat looking at each other for a brief moment, both very much aware of the other's presence.

CHAPTER 16

*T*he sky had turned cloudy and dark. The forecast had been confirmed. There was a bad storm ahead of them. It was not unusual weather this time of the year, for this area. The plane began to pitch about, an indication of strong winds outside.

John could sense Suzie was uneasy. This weather outside and the little storm brewing in her mind concerning this handsome young man beside her, was turning her first plane ride into quite an adventure, to say the least.

'I am getting uneasy. Is this unusual', she said, with a little panic in her voice.

John wanted to help, so he reached over and held her hand. The move shook her to her toes. She did not know how to handle the emotions overwhelming her.

CHAPTER 17

*A*t that moment, the lights went out for a second, coming back on somewhat dimmer. John knew they were the back-ups that ran off batteries. 'I'm going to the front to get some information as to what is happening', he said.

'Don't leave me, John, I am really frightened', she said. Her eyes were pleading with him, as she touched his arm. The reaction he felt was to hold her in his arms; to reassure this beautiful creature. But he knew that was out of the question.

'You are in no danger, Suzie', he assured her. 'I'll be right back. When the emergency lights came on, several things could have caused that. My concern is no announcement from the captain. Sit tight, I'll be back in a jiff', he smiled. The smile did the trick. Suzie relaxed in her seat.

He walked down the aisle and ran into a stewardess. 'The captain thinks we were hit by lightning, but everything is all right. You must return to your seat', she said.

CHAPTER 18

*H*e sat down next to Suzie and faced her. 'Everything is fine', he assured her, smiling, with all his concerns masked from his face. At that time, the plane came out of the clouds, but continued to be buffeted by winds. And John could tell it was losing altitude, slowly and steadily. This plane is headed for the ground, he thought, yet there was not a word from the cockpit.

He guessed all internal communications had been knocked out. The descent was another matter, though, and maybe all electric generation was gone, too. The crew must be too busy trying to keep the plane on a level flight, to let the passengers know what's happening, he pondered.

John told Suzie about the conversation with the stewardess. 'I think we may be headed for a forced landing', he said. Suzie reacted, looking him in the eyes.

'You mean we could crash, don't you', she said. There was no fear showing on her face. Anxiety, and concern, but with a little smile on her face. The calm and maturity she was displaying took John by surprise.

'Yes, there is that chance, and we must prepare ourselves for that possibility', he said.

CHAPTER 19

'The safest place on this plane is behind that back wall of the galley where the flight attendants prepare the hand-outs to us. Get all your stuff together: coat, overhead bag, etc, and all the blankets, and pillows you can carry and follow me', he said.

He showed her how to pull the bottom seat cushion out, as he reached down and loaded up with as many as he could hold, and ran to the rear of the plane. 'We must get as many of these as possible, but we have to hurry', he said.

After several trips, time was getting short, John thought. The plane was still headed down, when the engines stopped. Now John knew they were in trouble. He lined the floor in front of the rear wall of the galley, as well as the wall, also the outside wall.

'Lie down, Suzie. I'm going to cover you up with the rest of these cushions, then I'm going to lie on top of you. You must survive. You are too pretty to die', he said.

CHAPTER 20

Suzie lay on her back, looking into John's eyes. There was no fear showing on their faces, just inches apart. Suddenly, she put her arms around him and hugged him tightly. She released him, putting her hands on either side of his face, and kissed him full on the mouth.

'Oh, my', he said. He had never been kissed like that before, and surely never had he been so moved by a female. He knew instinctively, because of her age, he should not be doing this. But, his arms went around her, and he returned her kiss. Time stood still for them both. 'If I am to die, I want you in my arms', she whispered.

'Okay, but we have to put a cushion between our heads. Now, listen. If you survive, you are going to need shelter. The storm we went through is right behind us, and headed our way. It is a huge blizzard. A big and violent tempest. Good luck, princess', he said. As he positioned the padding, she kissed him again.

'I'm a Christian, John, and I don't fear death, but we are going to survive this because I have found the man I have dreamed of. I love you. If I don't live through this, then I hope to see you in heaven', she said.

'I am a Christian, Suzie, so I will see you later, no matter what', he uttered. 'We are going to see this through, young lady, so be careful what you say', he said.

'I mean it, John', she said. there was no doubt in her mind about her declaration of love for this man. Those were her last thoughts, as John pressed against her. 'I love you', she said.

CHAPTER 21

*H*e awoke and the first thought he had - Heaven? His last recollection was being thrown against the cushion on the bulkhead, and he blacked out. He felt for Suzie just as she stirred. Amazingly, they were close to the same place before the crash, and the floor was almost level. As he looked around, he could not see any damage in this area. He wondered how could that possibly be the case.

'Are you hurt?', he asked her.

'No, I'm fine', she answered as she moved next to John, and began to softly cry. 'We are alive', she said as she flew into his arms; sobbing, hugging, and kissing him. 'You saved us', she exclaimed, overcome with relief, joy, and love.

He wanted to return her caresses, but he knew from now on, he must refrain from physical contact with this underaged female, no matter how he felt. He would have to explain what his legal limits were concerning the law. All of those issues would have to come later, he thought.

'We have very pressing matters to deal with right now, Suzie. Bear with me. The first thing is to see if anyone else is alive', he said, as he smiled at her.

'Okay, John. Since you saved my life, I must obey your every command', she gleefully exclaimed. Her abrupt change, from a passionate woman, to the reality of their situation, made John shake his head in admiration of the young lady.

CHAPTER 22

*T*hey walked around the bulkhead to the entrance to the galley, and looked into the open sky, and empty space. The tail section where they were, had broken away from the front of the plane just about next to the forward bulkhead of the galley.

It was a fairly clean break, straight across, leaving an opening from the outside wall of the plane to the front wall of the galley. That would mean three seats, and the aisle, which was a little more than half the width of the plane. From where they were standing, they could see the wide swath, void of trees, where the rest of the plane had plowed through.

They were on the crest of a hill that fell away from them straight ahead, leaving them well above the rest of the plane. 'Let's see if we can open the outside door in the galley', John said.

After several pushes by both of them, the door opened. The ground was only about a foot down from the bottom of the plane.

They stepped out to see what had stopped this part of the plane, causing it to break apart, just in front of the galley wall. It was almost a clean break, leaving the opening less than the width of the fuselage. The hill sloped gradually away from the front edge of the plane.

'It will be easy to get in and out', he spoke to Suzie. 'We will block the opening in front where the plane broke apart with seat sections taken from the rear, and cushions stuffed in spaces to seal us from the coming storm', he said.

CHAPTER 23

*A*s they surveyed the rear section of the plane, John could see how it had not been ripped to pieces. It was wedged between two huge trees. They were just a couple feet further apart than the width of the plane.

'The pilot must have raised the nose of the plane just before impact to reduce their speed as much as possible. He dropped the tail section right down into that opening. Since the engines were on each side just in front of the ailerons, they rammed into the trees as it slid forward. This action caused the plane to break apart, and shear the heavy engines off, reducing the weight of the rear portion', he said.

'The sudden stop would have killed us if we had not been in our padded position. The metal bulkhead kept us from flying all over the place. We were very lucky', John said.

'Well, lucky for sure, but with God watching out for us, also. He has plans for us, John. I believe that', she said.

CHAPTER 24

'*I*'ve got to go down the hill and search for survivors. You stay here, and I'll be right back', he said.

'No, John, please don't leave me alone', she cried.

John explained the ruins would contain dead human beings, some in pieces. 'You will be able to see me from here. You can really help while I'm gone. We need to gather all the loose seat cushions. See, there is one over this way, and a couple to the left. We need every one we can find', John said.

He scanned the wreckage. He knew no one could have made it through that mess. There was total destruction scattered all down the hill and into the valley. Dozens of trees were mingled with pieces of the plane. There was a large section about 100 yards ahead. It looked as if it could be the nose portion, where the pilots would be.

'I'm going to walk down to that big chunk right over there', he pointed. 'You will be able to keep me in sight all the way. Keep looking for cushions, ok?', he said.

She nodded, as she continued her search. She knew he must leave her to do this searching, but there was a craving within her for this man's attention, and she did not know how to handle this new and wonderful feeling. She would have to keep busy and give her mind the time to adjust to this overwhelming emotion.

CHAPTER 25

She gathered all the cushions in a pile in front of doorway, doing what John had asked her to do. They had survived the crash, because he had foreseen what was coming. Suzie did not understand the urgency now, but she knew he had a reason. Looking down the hill, she could see him returning, carrying something big. As he got closer, she could tell it was a trunk.

'Everyone is dead. I tried to seal off the flight deck because the crew was relatively intact, and I didn't want wild animals getting to them. Nothing can be done for those all torn up and scattered. I am so glad we didn't have many people on board', he said.

Suzie could only stare out across the swath created by the plane. The thought of death for the others had not yet sunk into her mind, until now.

The realization had the effect of increasing her focus on John. The man had become the center of her life in the space of hours. She desperately needed for him to comfort and console her. The anxiety she was suffering must have registered in her facial expression, as John put his arm around her shoulder.

'I know this is so hard on you, Suzie, but we have a lot of work to do right now. We will have time later to rest. Everything is going to be all right, I promise', he said. The effect of his gesture and the words he spoke were enough for the young lady.

CHAPTER 26

*T*hey opened the trunk by breaking the lock with a stone. Much to his joy, it was full of tools. There was a large axe, just the thing John needed. Also, a ratchet set he would need to remove the attached seat sections where they had weathered the crash. John had already envisioned the need for clear space in this tail section of the plane.

John sat Suzie on one end of the trunk, and himself on the other facing her. 'I have not explained why I think we are in danger, Suzie. We came through a bad storm that knocked this plane down. Lightning must have destroyed the communication system completely. It probably fried most of the wires on the plane, knocking out some flight controls. We flew a long distance after that, which means the people on the ground have no idea where we are. I believe we are truly lost', he said.

'Judging by that dark sky over there, we crashed in a spot along the blizzard's path. The direction of the wind indicates it is coming this way. We have to prepare for that possibility by sealing the open part of this section of the plane. We have only a few hours to act', he said.

'How long do you think we have?', Suzie asked.

'We flew about a hundred miles after passing through the storm. This should give us about ten hours. I've got to go back down, and pick up everything we can use for our survival. If you will gather all the small branches, and loose wood and pile them where I'm standing. I will bring a bucket from the front galley, and fill it with fuel that is dripping from that wing section over to the right. We will build a bonfire. Nothing like a big blaze in the wilderness for the human spirit. It will be a beacon, in case anyone flies by', he said.

CHAPTER 27

*J*ohn headed where he found the trunk which was in the cargo container. It was busted open, but not totally destroyed. He had found two boxes he had to get up the hill. One of them contained duct tape. The other was full of new long-johns, tops and bottoms. He could not believe their good fortune. He remembered Suzie called it-'God's Will', not altogether luck.

Along with the tools in the trunk, John knew he had enough duct tape to weather-proof their refuge from the tempest. He fell to his knees, and thanked the Lord with his earnest prayer.

John brought the two boxes up the hill along with the can of fuel. He poured it on the wood, and started the fire. 'Wait until you see what we have found', he exclaimed, opening the cartons.

'This is duct tape, Suzie. It is a tough adhesive tape widely used in construction. We will wrap the cushions together, to form a mat the size of the opening in front. We will wedge seat sections between these rows next to the break, up to the ceiling in the aisle, and to the overhead bins over the seats. I'll tape them in place, and then put this curtain against the frames of the seat rows, taping it securely. I got the curtain from the first-class section. It will water-proof the opening.

Then I'll tape the mat of cushions next to the curtain, and it will help keep the cold out', he said.

John and Suzie worked together on the task. He used the tools he found to remove all the rows of seats in the back. He left two rows on the right of where the galley was. There remained an open area up to their barricade. 'I'm going to build a wood burning stove, and put it right here', he pointed.

'How are you going to do that?' she asked.

Trust me, I'm going to do it. I'll show you later. Right now, we have to tape these cushions together into a twin-sized mattress', he said.

He finished the job and placed it against the same bulkhead that had saved their lives. "This is where you will sleep, Suzie. With the blankets, pillows, and heavy coats we salvaged, it should be real cozy', he said.

'Where will you be, John?', she asked.

'I'll be in the front row, with the remainder of the cushions lining the back and bottom. It will be close to the stove, so everything will be fine', he said.

CHAPTER 28

'*I* told you earlier of my doubts about being found right away. I don't believe anyone has a clue where we crashed. If the blizzard hits us, we will be hidden under a huge blanket of snow and clouds, making it impossible to be spotted from the air. They have to be relatively close to pick up the black box signals, so if they are not looking in this area, it should be several days before they find us.

That is why we must have a secure place to be in, to survive', he said.

John must have noticed the slight smile on Suzie's face as he talked. He gave her a quizzical look. He could never have guessed what her smile was all about.

From the start, she thought they would be rescued right away. Maybe hours, but not days. She truly was in love with this man, but it would take time for any relationship to develop. If they were marooned, alone, and together, John would grow to love her in return, which was her desire and prayer. She felt God had answered her. 'Thank you, Lord. I know I am being selfish, and thinking only about myself, but I know You understand', she prayed.

'I have got to make a couple more trips down the hill', he said. 'Time is passing fast, and I have a lot to do. Keep the fire blazing, and will you start gathering small pieces of wood as close to the door as possible, but to the side, okay? I won't be long', he said.

CHAPTER 29

Suzie watched John walk away. She was grateful to have such a hard-working man looking out for her. She had been scared and alone just hours before. Now here she is in the middle of the wilderness, with a storm about to descend on them. What was a sixteen-year-old girl to think of her future.

Well, right now, her 'future' was headed back with his arms full. 'We continue to be blessed, and extremely lucky, Suzie. I got into the baggage container and found these sleeping bags. They are three of them and they are cold-weather goodies.

With the long-johns and these items, we will be warm as toast. I have another journey to make. And I found our checked luggage', he said. The last item he had to bring up was a door from the first-class area. 'I will build a stove from its parts', he added.

'It will be a crudely constructed one, but it will keep us from freezing. The door is two sheets of metal, held apart with a honeycomb, cardboard center, glued together. I am going to take the center out, leaving the metal. I'll bend one sheet two times. the middle area will be the width of the sheet, sitting flat on the ground, with the sides sticking up. I'll off-set the bends on the other sheet, so that one side is longer than the other, with the middle the same width as the first.

Nesting one on top of each sheet gives me a four-sided enclosure. I'll bend the long side of the off-set sheet down toward the closure, and I have stove, with an opening on one side where the short side is. The louver in the door will be on the top part of the sheet, and by removing it, I have an opening for my chimney. I have a whole bunch of wire from the plane I'll use to wrap the stove many times, securing "L" shaped strips on the seams with the wire. I punch some holes in the bottom for ventilation', he said. He finished and mounted it on four flat rocks, one on each corner.

They started a fire, and it worked great. A little smoky, but not too much.

CHAPTER 30

'Oh, John, we have a fire', Suzie exclaimed. Her enthusiasm was overwhelming as she grabbed John in a bear-hug. The gesture was beautiful and sweet, and it took his breath away, leaving him speechless.

They were face to face. John could see the love in her eyes. John wondered if she could see the longing in his. Her smile gave him the answer. He put his arms around her, and they kissed lightly. He knew he had to keep things under control, he reminded himself.

'Suzie, we have a lot of work to do, so we need to get with it', he said with a wink. 'We need to have lots of wood inside before the storm gets here', he said.

He pointed toward the ominous blackness creeping across the mountains. He was trying to divert everything away from this beautiful, but dangerous young lady in front of him. Dangerous for him, but there could not be any contact with her, other than a hug and kiss.

'Once we get prepared for this blizzard, we will have lots of time to talk and get acquainted', he said. 'Right now, I need your help. You have been so good. I am amazed how grown-up you have been. We just need a few more hours', he said.

'Okay, tell me what to do', she answered, with a return smile.

'First, I will build a lean-to against the plane, just back of the door, by propping a row of those logs over there. I'll trim them except for the tops, and stack limbs on them. That will give us a shelter to put the logs I am cutting. These will be extra.

We will have the rear of the plane full as much as we can. I don't want to dig in the snow out here, if we run out of wood inside. We need to leave walking space back to the latrines, and for me to have room to cut logs small enough to fit into the stove', he said.

CHAPTER 31

*H*e lit the bonfire, and soon it was roaring. There is nothing more soothing to humans than a big fire, John thought. Especially to these two, basking in its warmth. They stood together for a few moments, savoring each other's presence.

They worked hard gathering the wood. Suzie carried the smaller pieces inside, while John hacked and sawed the longer ones. It was tiring labor, and John could see that Suzie was worn out.

'We have got it almost completed. I have to make a trip down the hill to bring back one more item. Please go inside and lie on the bed, Suzie. I'll only be a few minutes', he said, smiling broadly at the young lady.

Suzie was exhausted, but she was not going to leave, not until John returned from his trek. She could see the clouds were much closer and very dark. The wind had begun to blow, and it was noticeably colder. 'I am tired, John, but I'll take these logs while you're gone', she said.

Suzie kept her eyes on the young man, who had been a stranger such a short time ago. Now, it seemed her every thought centered on him. It had been really hard for her not to embrace him, as they stood before the blaze earlier. She even felt a little anger toward him for not initiating some show of affection for her.

She had that confident assurance all pretty young women have when it comes to knowing how their beauty attracts men. She knew John was well aware of her feeling for him, and could not fully understand his reluctance.

'I want him to love me', she prayed. Then, she thought how selfish it was to ask the Lord for something like that. We are alive, she reminded herself. She had no experience to fall back on, to give her guidance as how to handle her emotions.

There had to be a reason John seemed to be avoiding any physical contact with her. Maybe he had a girlfriend he was in love with. She knew one thing for sure, though. Such thoughts were not going to help, so she resolved that her focus would be cheerful, and confident.

No man alive can resist me. You are a dead duck, John Stevens, she thought, as she burst out laughing. She couldn't believe how her mind was working, right now. It had been a long time since she had wanted any male attention. She had stopped dating last year, when it became clear boys her age had no clues to what her needs were. All they seemed to care about were their own desires.

Now this encounter with a male was a totally new experience. Very different, indeed, she thought. She wondered how it would progress, as they would be alone, together in a very intimate situation. She had continued collecting wood as her mind pondered her future, and she realized she was very tired.

Just then, John came up the hill. He noticed the fatigue on her face, and led her inside.

'Suzie, it will be dark shortly and the storm is close. You really must lie down and rest. We can't allow you to wear yourself down like this. It has been wonderful the way you have worked', he exclaimed.

Tears came to Suzie's eyes as John expressed his concern for her. She was so desperate in need of TLC, this little show of affection got to her. John took her into his arms, lifted her face up, and kissed her softly, and tenderly. 'We will have plenty of time tomorrow to talk, Suzie, and get to know one another. Get to sleep, pretty lady, and I'll see you later', he said.

A smile came to her face.

'That was what I needed the most, John. Now, I can rest in peace. Hey, I didn't mean that literally. I should have said, I will peacefully rest', she laughed.

CHAPTER 32

*J*ust as they parted, a cool breeze whistled in amongst the trees, the signal the blizzard was really near. Suzie walked into their safe haven, and spread out on the bed.

Although exhausted, she did not think sleep would come easily. Yet, only seconds later, she was sound asleep.

John gathered an arm load of wood and entered where Suzan lie. He took a couple blankets and put them on the sleeping young girl. He had never seen such a lovely sight. God was indeed great, and he thanked Him for sparing their lives.

He hoped he was right about their rescue being days away. They were safe now for awhile, so let it snow, let snow, let it snow! He needed some quiet time with this person.

He finished gathering the wood he had cut, just as the wind began to blow much harder, and it was colder. He looked at his watch and noted it was almost midnight. He headed for the door, closing it tightly.

He walked by Suzie toward the stove to check on his wall. Very little wind was getting in, and he put cushions and tape to seal those cracks. The direction of the breeze was from the rear and then the snow arrived. He could not see it, but he could hear it against the back of the plane.

CHAPTER 33

Suzie woke with a jolt. The wind was really howling, and fear was in her eyes. From the light of the fire, she could see John seated next to the stove.

He heard her move and came around to sit next to her on the pads. 'You were sleeping so well', he said as he held her hands. 'Don't worry. The storm has arrived full force, and everything is holding together. We are safe. Our labors have paid off, and our prayers have been answered', he said.

'How long have I been asleep?', she asked.

'It is past two o'clock. You must be hungry', he said.

She shook her head and tears came to her eyes. This time because she felt so good. 'You have saved my life again. For the second time in one day, I am alive because of your foresight, John', she said.

'God seems to like us, Suzie. I want to pray with you', as he knelt beside her. The moment was both reverent, and emotional as they gave thanks to the Lord.

'I have a pot of hot water on the stove. We can have coffee, tea, or hot chocolate', John offered. 'I don't want anything', she said.

John could tell something was bothering the young lady. He felt he knew the reason, because he sensed a heavy tension between them. When two people share an intimate a kiss and embrace as they had, and there is an exclamation of love, there can not be a casual attitude, no matter the circumstances. John was unsure how he should handle things. On one hand, he needed to assure Suzie her affections were wanted, and even desired by him.

However, there was this problem of the age difference between them. As an adult, he could have no physical, sexual contact with this underage girl. A kiss and a hug might be alright, but nothing beyond that. He felt Suzie was taking his actions toward her as a rejection.

'We are both tired, Suzie. We have had a long hard day. Tomorrow, we have nothing but time. I am not going anywhere, and neither are you. I want you to know how much I admire you, young lady', he said as he held her hands. 'We are in a volatile situation, the two of us. I want you to put on a couple sets of these long-johns over your underwear. I'll do the same. We will be fully clothed, for warmth. Would you be offended if I slept next to you, for warmth? I hope you trust me, Suzie', he said.

She looked him in the eye and nodded. Her heart was beating so fast, she could not speak. His words had overcome her. Everything was 'right', in her world. Just one act from this man, and she felt she was in heaven. She loved him. No question in her mind about it..

The broad grin on Suzie's face was the answer he was looking for. John knew that this sweet, pretty lovely female was his partner. Not in sex, but in companionship. What did the smile have to do with his conclusion?

John had remembered their encounter just before the crash. Suzie had told him of her Christian faith. Her belief in Jesus Christ would not allow her to commit a sin without it tearing at her soul. If she had resigned to being immoral with him, it would have been with a heavy heart, and it would have shown on her face, no matter how much she loved him. She believed he was a Christian, and the request he made because he loved her, not lusted for her. Therefore, the broad grin, instead of a somber face.

CHAPTER 34

*J*ohn's return smile cemented their faith in each other. They would handle all the problems that could be generated by their situation. He looked forward to learning more about this beautiful woman.

CHAPTER 35

$\mathcal{H}$e had heard of blizzards of this type lasting days, so they could be here some time. John couldn't recall if he had told Suzie about finding the deer carcass in the wreak debris. He had skinned it, and cut three large chunks, carrying them up the hill in a bucket he found in the first-class galley. John was brought back to the present by Suzie calling him. 'I'm sorry, I was day-dreaming', John said.

Suzie had snuggled in her sleeping bag and was telling him goodnight. 'I am so tired. See you later', she said.

John sat in the light of the blazing fire, gazing down at the young lady, his mind recounting the events of the day. Others have had their 'longest day', and after this one, he could understand why they would call it that. And this woman has been a huge part of it all. He had started a daily journal in law school, to record day-to-day activities, and he now took the time to bring it up to date. He pondered his status, and knew the one big danger he faced, had to be his conduct with Suzie Wells. His actions with her would be the main interest of the world, when they were rescued. The questions would be many and pointed. To some, he had already crossed the line.

Their kisses and hugs had been intense, but understandable, due to the circumstances.

There's only one way he could handle this. He would not answer any questions regarding his interactions with Suzie. Total silence. He would advise Suzie of his decision, and it would be up to her how she handled her side of matter. He knew they would not go beyond hugs and kisses. A look, a smile, a hand-squeeze. It would have to suffice.

As he prepared to join Suzie in sleep, John reflected on his feeling for Suzie. All his emotions at first had been a male protecting a female. Well, not all, he thought. She was a real beauty, and she looked so much like his late sister, Jeanie. His feelings were changing, this was for sure. He had never been in love, and never had this gut-wrenching reaction toward a woman. He was falling in love, and it made him really happy. He felt like waking her and confessing to her how he felt, but knew he could not say those words. Maybe he shouldn't tell her at all. Right now, he was too tired to think straight as he started to lie down next her, but decided to sleep on the seats near the fire. He rationalized his actions would disturb her. Those were his thoughts as he fell asleep.

CHAPTER 36

John slowly came out of the best sleep he had enjoyed since the accident that claimed his family. He sat up, and saw Suzie seated in the row in front of him next to the fire. She heard the movement behind her and turned around.

'Good morning, John. I put a couple logs in the stove, and the fire is really cooking. The wind is much stronger and it is colder this morning', she said.

'How long have you been awake?', he asked.

'Oh, about an hour. I woke up expecting to feel you by me, but I couldn't find you. Why did you sleep up here?', she asked with a pouty look on her face.

'You were sleeping so soundly, I was afraid I would disturb the sleeping beauty, so serene and peaceful. People tell me I sometimes snore, especially when I'm real tired. So, I crashed here', he said.

'It will be a lot colder tonight, and we will need all the cover we can find, so make room for me, Suzie', he said.

'No one ever called me Suzie. I like it', she exclaimed, with a wide grin. She knew he was attempting to ease any tension. Since his remark about tonight's sleep arrangements, everything was fine with her.

John took his bag up to where Suzie was seated and moved next to her. He pulled the arm-rest between them out of the way.

They were side-by-side, each in their separate sleeping bags. John was drinking coffee, and Suzie was having hot cocoa. The storm was raging outside, but they were warm and cozy.

John noticed ice was forming at a crack in the wall that covered the open front of the plane section.

'I've got to close that place where the ice is', he said, pointing ahead. Suzie watched him work, and silently said a word of prayer, thanking the Lord for her wonderful good fortune. She was so proud of him, admiration showing on her face. He had kept them alive, and as he came back to his seat, tears came to her eyes. 'You must think I'm a big cry-baby. Well, I'm not. It overwhelms me when I see what you have done to protect us', she said.

'Don't you forget all you have done, Suzie. None of this would have been completed but for your help. All of this was us busting our butts, together', he smiled as he drew her into his arms.

There was so much they had to talk about, but right now, they relaxed in an embrace. He could tell Suzie was tired. Although she slept well, yesterday had been so full of stress, and a very long day. She let her head rest on his shoulder, as sleep caught up with her. John pulled their bags close, and joined her in a needed rest.

John woke to the roar of a howling tempest. He could never have imagined such a storm. It was colder, windier, and the snow was really coming down.

He moved to stoke the fire, waking Suzie. Panic showed in her eyes for a second, until she felt John beside her. She realized she had fallen asleep, because she was refreshed.

'We are in the midst of one bad blizzard. I couldn't guess how cold it is, but I fear it will be even worse later on. I have read about these storms in this area lasting days, and this one could be a record-breaker', he said.

'I get scared when I think of where we would be now, if you had not foreseen this coming, John', she said. The sweet look on her beautiful face melted his heart.

'Suzie, let's take this time to get to know each other better, he said.

'Okay, I want to start, because I really need for you to understand about my life up to now', she began.

'Up until a year or so ago, I was a teenager growing in a normal family. I am an only child, and the apple of my father's eye. He was a successful business owner, and a wonderful parent. I adored him. I know you have noticed my reference to him is in the past tense. He died suddenly, tearing my world asunder', she said.

'We were very close, much to the chagrin of my mother. She is a socialite, and makes no bones about her priorities. Being a loving mother was not one of them. We tolerated each other. Dad and I were Christians, while mom went along with the church-going more as a charade-sort of. You know the type Christianity she professed. Every church has a few. Dad and I never mentioned it. He would always invite her to come along with us to the services, but she mostly had something else to do', she said.

'I withdrew from everything, except the Church, after he died. I stopped dating before that, mainly because I could not find a decent guy I liked. My actions created the impression in school I was a conceited stuck-up, rich, pretty student. I couldn't help it, John. To make matters worse, Mother began seeing this man, almost immediately.

I felt this was a dishonor to my father's memory, and I told her so', she said. "Her answer stressed he was gone, and life went on. I am sure she knew this Bill Sloan before. They hooked up pretty fast. So fast, they were married about six months later. I was disgusted with both of them, and I withdrew even more', she said.

'My everyday living got worse in a hurry', she sobbed. Tears streaming down her face, as she recalled what happened next. 'Bill tried from the start to be friendly with me, but I despised the man, both for what I thought was a slap at my father, and the open way he ogled me from the beginning. I know I am attractive, John, but for a couple years, I have gone out of my way to down-play my appearance, and especially to that guy. One day, he grabbed me and began assaulting me. I broke free and ran down the street to the house of my father's friend, Mr. Owens.

'He was dialing the police, when my mother arrived and asked him not to call. She said she would handle it, and Mr. Owens hung up. He looked at me for help as to how to proceed.

I didn't know what to do, John. I was frightened, but I felt safe then, so I didn't object when mother led me away. I know now that was a huge mistake, because as soon as we got home, mother began accusing me of enticement toward her husband. She even said I had been doing this before', as she spoke through her tears.

John held her as she moaned, as recalling those days tore at her heart. 'Mother told me she had called Dad's family up north, and arranged for me go live with them. She gave the excuse of the death of my father had completely changed me, and I needed to be around his kinfolk. I knew I could never be comfortable around either of those two, so I welcomed the move, but only for the one reason. I had never been away from the only home I had ever known. I was scared to death, John. Now you know why I was on this plane, alone. I was frightened, but I was glad to be apart from those people', she said.

'I prayed a lot, asking for God's guidance. I believe He has answered my prayers, John. You are aware I believe all this is with His blessings. He abides in my heart, and He listens to his children. We are together, at this moment, because we have placed our loves in His hands', she said in a low voice barely audible above the wind.

CHAPTER 37

*J*ohn was almost in shock as he listened to Suzie talk. It was a heart-rendering account of the worst case of child abuse he had ever heard of. His law training took hold of his thought processes. He began to realize just how much this treatment festered on this young lady, and would impact both their lives.

'Right now, your folks are most likely celebrating the news that your plane is missing, and has probably crashed. With the storm blowing over the area where it would have gone down, they are hearing reports no one could have survived both the crash and the bad weather. They must feel they are free of any repercussion from their actions against you' John said.

Your estate will be awarded richly for your demise, and your mother is your parent, which means she gets everything. Oh, I'll bet they are putting on quite a scene about losing their darling daughter. The more they act, the more they will react to you being found safe and sound. Suzie, I will explain later, why their reaction will be so important to us'.

'I won't comment a lot on what you just told me. I am so angry about your treatment, and what you have gone through. They have hurt you, but I am betting that you do not seek revenge. That pretty smile tells me I am right. You have survived and you will return. Let's make certain your return will be a triumphant one, sweet lady", he said.

CHAPTER 38

'*I* want to tell you about myself', he started. 'I had my 21st birthday a couple months ago. Which means I am an adult male. I mention that, because it is a very important fact in regards to our relationship-both present and future. Present-since you are a minor female, I am in danger of being sent to prison if I initiate any contact with you considered inappropriate', he said.

'You know what happened to you at the hands of your stepfather was most assuredly a criminal act. Well, even my kissing you would be, also, if I did not have your permission to do so. But, it could be used against me, anyhow. I mention this, Suzie, to help explain any hesitation on my part toward you. You are the most attractive female I have ever known. Put that together with your sweet disposition, and your Christian faith makes you almost irresistible', he said. 'Please remember those facts, when I show you this snapshot, young lady', he said.

John pulled a picture from his wallet and handed it to Suzie. When she saw that it was a photograph of a young female, her heart skipped a beat. Was this a picture of his girlfriend, she thought, or even his wife?

Then she took a closer examination. 'John, who is this girl', she said. 'She looks a lot like me. We have the same hair style and color, and the identical shape of our face', she said.

John held her hand as he introduced the young lady as his deceased sister, Debbie. 'I could not tell you the real reason I lost it when we first met. It was the resemblance of you two that really floored me. I had not gotten a good look at you at the beginning when I walked toward you on the plane. Debbie and I were closer than most siblings, so losing her along with mom and dad almost brought me to my knees', he said.

'If I had known you, I would have commented at the time about how much you look like her. So, I blamed my discomfort at the moment entirely on the accident, when it was mostly the shock of your appearance which caused my reaction. How does it make you feel, knowing the impact you have had on me?', he said, with a smile on his face.

CHAPTER 39

*N*ow, Suzie was presented with a new worry. Was John's interest in her due to the look-a-like between herself and Debbie? Already their age difference stood in their way, but such a problem will be taken care of in a couple years when I reach 18, she thought.

After pondering the question about Jeanie for a while, she eased her anxiety by coming to the conclusion that John would be repelled from any relationship with his sister's look-a-like, if he even thought there was a connection of his feelings toward either woman. He loved his sister as a sibling, and he would not love her as a woman, she surmised. Now, I must have his love. 'God willing, make him be mine', she prayed.

'John', she said. 'In answer to your question about how I feel about me impacting you, this is how I feel'. She moved as close as she could to him, putting her arms around his shoulders. There were six or seven layers of clothes between them, but their contact was electric; their kiss was breathe-taking. 'I know you spoke of our not doing this', she sighed. 'I have never felt better, though' she said.

John's reaction was one of compassion, not lust. A nice glow of light and warmth amidst the cold and gloom of their situation. He knew nothing bad or forbidden would be allowed to happen between them. They sat together as John talked about his past.

Finally, he said: 'That is my life, Suzie. No one to come home to. No girl-friend, just a lot of friends back home', he said.

CHAPTER 40

John stoked the fire, and got it blazing hot. By sitting close to it, they could feel the warmth. And they needed it, because it was getting colder, and they also needed to eat. John had put a chunk of the venison in a pot of tomato soup on the stove earlier and it was as close to beef stew as he could get it. 'Not bad', he said as he handed Suzie a spoon-full.

She grimaced. 'A little wild tasting, but I'm hungry and it will do fine', she said. They ate, and giggled together, comfortable with the food and each other, while the storm increased its fury. Their second day was coming to an end. The only way they knew it was night-time, was by the watch John had on his wrist. There was no sunshine or light coming through the blizzard.

'I would like to know just how cold it is', John said. 'Come to think about it, maybe we don't need to know. It would probably freak us out if we knew.

Ignorance is bliss, so they say', he said.

CHAPTER 41

'We have two choices on how we spend this night', John said. We can huddle here near the fire in these seats, or we can combine all our sleeping-bags and blankets and sleep on our home-made mattress close together. I suggest we each put another layer of long-johns on, and we should be comfortable'. What do you say, Princess?

'The bed', she said.

'Okay, I have an alarm on my watch, which I will set it for two hours. That way, we can keep the fire going. We'll move up close to these seats, which puts us closer to the stove, but far enough away to be safe', he said.

They started out lying face to face, so they could talk. The blankets and sleeping-bags muffled the noise of the wind, allowing them to hear each other. This was a new experience for both of them to be in a bed as they were.

'We are both nervous, I can tell', John said.

'No, I am not', Suzie spoke up. 'You are, John Stevens. And I just realized that you are afraid of me, Kind Sir. Don't be, because I bid you no harm, sweet Prince. You are in good hands', as she wrapped both arms around him. 'Sleep tight. I'll keep the boogie-man away from you', she whispered. 'I'm going to turn over now. The move will let us snuggle. Goodnight, John', she said aloud, and softly added to herself-'sweetheart'.

CHAPTER 42

*J*ohn bade the young lady a goodnight and he lay there, unable to sleep. He could tell by her breathing, that she was in dreamland. It made him relax, feeling her so comfortable in this situation. She was such a confidant woman, and he truly had to recognize her as such, and not a teen-ager, at least in her maturity of thought and action. He promised himself again that he was not going to mess up this wonderful thing going for them right now. He thanked the Lord for his blessings - and slept.

His watch brought him awake. It was not very loud, and Suzie slept through it, but came awake when she felt him start to get up by pulling away from their snuggle.

'What's wrong?', she said.

'Everything is alright', he answered. 'It's time to fix the fire. I'll be only a few minutes', he said. 'Okay, don't be long. I'll keep the bed warm', she said. 'Can I continue to be so lucky', he thought.

Just two days into this new life, out in the wilderness, with a howling storm threatening to devour us, and we don't have a care in the world. 'Well, maybe a little worry here and there', he thought. He could tell the blizzard had gotten stronger, and it was colder.

The fire was back going full blast, which was not making much of a dent inside. So much for our full famous stove, John wondered. But, it was some help in the heat department, much more so in the feel-good aspect, plus heating water, and cooking our deer meat.

CHAPTER 43

S uzie called to him. 'Get back in here, and keep me warm', she said. He slid into the sleeping-bag, and was greeted with a nice hug. 'It is getting worse out there. We may have to put on those heavy parkas when we get up. I have never heard such wind', he said.

'We don't have to worry about anyone reaching us for at least a few days', Suzie said out loud, and a thank-you, to herself. I could easily turn into a conniving female, she thought.

They settled down in their bed, and Suzie once again fell asleep. John marveled at how fast she did it. Just like a little baby, she sought warmth and security, and found both as she drew soft and easy breathes.

Again, John was aroused by the alarm. This time, he was careful not to disturb Suzie. 'I'm going to have to let this fire die down, instead of keeping it going', he thought. 'Better to get a full sleep', was his reasoning.

CHAPTER 44

*T*hey woke to the same roar of the storm, but they did not notice. 'I will never forget this night', Suzie said. 'I hope they never find us'.

'Don't wish that', John said. 'Let's not tempt fate. Wish for about a week more. You will probably get awfully sick of this place by then. While you were telling me of your encounter with your step-father, I began considering what your folk's reaction could be when we are rescued. They are going to try to discredit anything you said. 'Let's get up, have something to eat, and I'll discuss this with you later', John said.

CHAPTER 45

*T*hey began their third day with hot beverages. The coffee and hot chocolate were warming, and delicious, and refreshing. They were seated next to the stove, and the heat from the fire could be felt. And it sure was a welcome feeling.

'I'm going to have to do a little work', John said. 'I saved the covers off the backs of the seats. They slip right up, and are in one piece. I'm going to cut the stitches out, and we will have a flat piece of cloth. I will duct tape enough together to make a blanket. I have some wire left, and I'll weave the wire into the top of the blankets, and we will have a curtain. I'll mount it behind this row of seats we are sitting on, from the outside wall of the plane, to the galley bulkhead, closing in the stove. That should warm this area very well', he said.

John and Suzie labored on this project for several hours, and finally finished. 'Now, Suzie, I'm rolling in this cart from the galley. I have taken everything off, and now I put the two pans of water on the stove, and roll it next to this side of the stove, pointing to the left. Here's a couple towels, a wash rag, and soap from the lavatory. I found our luggage in the wreckage, and here is yours. I'll put it on one of the seats, so you can get into it. You, my young lady, can take a bath. I would suggest you do the top first. Dry off, and put these clean clothes on, then do the bottom.

What do you think about that, he said. 'While you bathe, I will cut some of these long logs, so they will fit in the stove. You are completely enclosed, giving you total privacy', so have at it', he said.

This was almost too much for Suzie to grasp. Last night, she had begun to worry about her hygiene, fearful of having her body giving out an offensive odor. She stood now, in this small warm spot, getting ready to become clean again. All because of this man, another problem in her life was solved.

Suzie finished the bath, and put a pretty dress she had in the suitcase over the clean long-johns. She got her make-up and put on her 'face'. She combed her hair, and put on high-heeled shoes. And stepped out of the closure. John was facing her as she emerged. The light of the fire was at her back, making it hard for John to see everything, but the dress stood out. And her silhouette was breathtaking.

He dropped the axe and walked toward her. She giggled, and John laughed out loud.

'Now, I've seen everything. Here we are, stuck in the wilderness, and you look like you are ready to go dancing. May I have this dance, pretty lady?', he said.

'It will have to be a slow one, and no jitter-bugging', she laughed, as they did a little two-step. 'I feel like a woman again, John. Having a bath, and my face fixed, with a dress on, with high heels. But most of all, having a man admire me. Thank you so much', she cried.

'We are so lucky for a lot of reasons, Suzie. All of them matter, but the really big one is we, you and I, survived together', he said. 'Nothing can happen that will ever erase our memories of these past days, or the impact everything has had on our lives. I truly look forward to whatever lies ahead for us. I say 'us', because we are forever linked together by these events', he said.

'We have a future, you and I, and how much of a future is 'us', I wonder.

John knew that Suzie felt that she loved him, and with all they had gone through together, she would want him to have the same feeling for her. No matter how he felt about her, he must play it down. He had to give her the option of being able to rethink her feelings once we got out of this situation. She is so young to have had to experience all of this, he thought. Well, if we have a few more days here, maybe the time together in such a stressful relationship will solidify both our feelings.

CHAPTER 46

*S*uzie sensed a reluctance toward her. She could think of several reasons for his emotions, and wondered how she should react. She had noticed intensely every interaction they had experienced. There was no doubt in her mind that he was attracted to her. When she thought about why he felt that way, the picture of his sister came to her mind. She had decided before that the similarities between herself and Debbie were a plus for her.

Her comment to him that he was afraid of her, had not been challenged. Her intentions in mentioning that was more kidding than serious, but she did feel there was some truth in it. The extent of his reaction to her was in her hands, however. How she handled herself was so important, she thought. Lucky for her, she did not have to put on an act. No flirting, or using her beauty to overwhelm the man. Just tell him how you feel, and everything will be fine, were her thoughts. 'I have told him before of my love for him, and I'll do it again-and again'.

CHAPTER 47

*S*he went back by the stove and took the dress off, and the makeup, and the shoes. It had been fun, but now reality time, she thought. She put a couple logs on the fire, as John knocked.

'Can I come in', he asked.

'I'm in my three sets of long-johns, so I think I'm covered pretty well', she answered. 'I'm going to bathe now, so get fully dressed, because it is getting colder. I wish I had a thermometer. It has to be 20 below or worse. Let's move our bed where the cart is, for tonight.

The heat from the stove will help keep us warmer, and this enclosed area will be heated much better', he said.

John finished his 'bath', shaved with his razor from his luggage, and got all slicked up, just for Suzie, he thought. He told her to come in, and there they stood. Two clean, happy, young people, staring into each other's eyes.

'Much better, huh', John said.

'Yeah, much better', she answered, and hugged him as she planted a kiss on his lips. There was love in her countenance and John reacted, as she backed away a half step. 'Let's get our seats fixed, because you need to tell me about my mother's reaction you mentioned before', she said.

'Holy mackerel, the woman is going to kill me', he thought. but, in his heart, he thanked her. Right then and there, John realized his life was in her hands. "Gladly, I accept my fate, you gorgeous creature', he thought.

CHAPTER 48

*B*y getting into one sleeping-bag, and pulling the hood around their faces, a lot of the noise from the wind was blocked out. Talking was a lot easier, and it sure was nice and snug.

'You recall, I started to tell you what your parent's reactions could be when they learn of your rescue. As I said, they will be knocked for a loop when they hear you are alive and well. I think they will fight back by trying to discrediting you. They have to establish the fact you are a delinquent, thus it was your actions that caused your step-father to act as he did. They will assure the world of that fact, by accusing us of sexual misconduct while we were marooned together', John said.

'It is one thing to accuse, and another to prove that. And this how I think she will try to do it. She will demand you be given a rape examination, as soon as they can get you to a hospital. Any activity in or around your 'privates' can be detected several ways. Through penetration, and DNA present on your body', he said.

'Since I am the only one here, I would immediately be arrested for molesting a minor female. It would not matter if any such acts were done with your approval. I would be at fault. Now, the fact that you took baths, while marooned, could wash any DNA away, but it would not affect any sexual penetration, just cloud the issue somewhat. The only complete exoneration would come from the examination showing you are a virgin', he said.

'John, I took enough sex education in school to know what you are talking about. My dad started preparing me for puberty when I was 12 years old. He wanted me to know the facts of life, so to speak, and be ready for the change in my body, and my mind', she said.

'Our church also taught the value and worth of our body, both boys and girls. I stopped dating almost from the start, because I found I gained nothing from it, just clumsy attempts from inept boys. I limited my social activities to within the church, and developed some wonderful friendships, with both boys and girls.

John, I am a virgin, and will remain so until I marry', she said.

CHAPTER 49

'That is good to know, young lady. That settles it from that angle. Now the question is, your mother is your guardian, with complete control over you because of your age. You will need legal counsel on that item, and on the disposition of your father's estate. You did tell me you received nothing, is that correct? Okay, I am an attorney, and will act in your behalf, but you must hire me. There is no fee involved, but you have to ask me to be your lawyer', he said.

'Will you be my attorney, Mr. John Stevens?', she asked.

'Good! The first thing I will have to do on your behalf, is to ask you if my grandmother, Ann Stevens, would be acceptable, to be named your guardian', John said. 'She lives alone in my family's home. Well, it is now my home. Her husband died several years ago, and I am now her only living relative. I will call her as soon as we are rescued. Jeanie was her favorite. They talked nearly every day. Grandma moved to a retirement home two years ago. When I asked her to move into the family home, she was thrilled. I have a full-time nurse living with her, and she says I saved her life. The loss of her son and granddaughter almost killed her', John said.

'You will make her life complete, Suzie. It is very important that you have a home to go to, after we leave here. The social services of either this state, or your home one, will try to take custody of you, if you refuse to go back to your parents. We want to offer an alternative, and my grandmother will fill the bill; that is, if you agree', he said.

'You may, someday, know how happy you have made me feel, John, asking me to be a part of your family. I certainly, with all my heart, would welcome that happening. John, in reality, I am alone in this world. And I need your love, along with a home. I'm not begging or asking for anything. I just need for you to know I truly love you', she said.

'These past few days have opened my eyes and mind to the need everyone really has for 'family'. I lost mine when my dad died. I thought of looking for a man to help replace him, John. It would have been so easy, I reckoned, to get married and hope for the best. I knew it would get me away from the torment I was in, regarding my parents' attitude toward me. When the incident with my stepfather happened, I regretted not taking such action. I have had this adventure with you, however, to make me realize how foolish and reckless that would have been. John, I am not in a reckless mood right now. God, and you are directing my life, and believe me when I say-I love you. I would love to have her as my guardian', she said.

CHAPTER 50

'*I* want you to remember what you just said, Suzie', John said. 'You realize now that sometimes wrong choices are made, especially when we are under stress.

Please believe me when I tell you this. My concern for you is this storm! Maybe I should have said; wait out this storm, before we make life-long decisions about our lives', he said.

'We have a few days left together here before they find us, at the least. Then our real moments of truth will begin. If I do my job as your attorney correctly, I must not take my personal feelings into account. Everyone following our adventure will be looking for signs of our attraction to each other. It will give them clues about our conduct while marooned together on this desert island. I must not show that I am head-over-heels in love with you. I must not look at you as the beautiful woman you are, but as a client, devoid of all those many charms', he said.

'My goodness!', he proclaimed. 'Who am I kidding. Suzie, I have fallen in love with you. It's been coming on ever since I met you. I cannot conceal my feelings right this moment, and I could not in front of the world. I'll just have to cope with that handicap, and hope for my best', he said.

They were snuggled in the sleeping bags by the fire, so all Suzie could do was embrace John, and give him a tear stained kiss. His announcement was welcomed, but did not come as a big surprise.

She was not experienced in men falling in love with her, but she had wished, and willed, and prayed this man would. And all her anxious pleas were coming to pass.

'I know you worry about this, John', she whispered. 'We have a long way to go in learning of each other's personalities, and likes and such and I know we have a tough wait until I am of age, before we can really think of our future', she said.

CHAPTER 51

*J*ohn hushed her, by returning her kiss. 'It is one thing to tell a person of your love, and another for there to be assumptions of other 'things' to follow', he said. Just so we don't get confused about what our love for each other gives us, I am going to do this'. He turned in his seat, falling to his knees against Suzie's legs. He took her hands in his, and put them next to his heart.

'Suzie, I am both of sound mind, and in love with you. I want to spend my life with you by my side. Will you marry me, please?', he asked.

Years later, Suzie knew she would remember every moment; every emotion of this. There were going to be more such occasions like this, she was sure of, but right now, her whole being was alive with pure ecstasy. She got as close to John as possible, but with all the clothes and sleeping bag and blankets, it was not real intimate. It was enough, and she put his face in her hands. She kissed him, and said, 'I will'.

CHAPTER 52

*T*hey were not in the mood for food at this time, but their bodies were demanding attention. John built up the fire as Suzie brought the meal from the galley. They talked, and ate, and cuddled, with more talk and cuddles than eating. When it was over, John returned everything to the galley. He returned shortly, with two glasses full of a red liquid.

'I picked up one bottle of red wine from the first -class section', John said. 'I don't think we should drink more than this glass-full. In our state of mind, we are almost intoxicated as it is. So, we will toast ourselves to our engagement, and our lives together, and hope we don't get roaring drunk', he said.

They crossed their arms, and brought the glasses to their lips. It was a touching moment for them both. Neither one had ever been in love, much less engaged. 'I sure wish we had a camera for this', John said.

'It will always be burned in my memory', Suzie said, as they drank together.

'Wow, I better not have anymore. No telling what I might do, under the influence, so to speak', he said.

'Me, too. Let's resume this after our wedding, shall we?', she said.

'Okay, love of my life', he murmured in her ear.

CHAPTER 53

*T*he day had passed, and they could hear the wind tearing against the make-shift wall in front of them. But it all held together, much to their comfort. 'We'll get extra warmth being this close to the stove, and inside the curtain area. I'll bank the fire as much as I can, and still be safe. The do-it-yourself contraption is holding up fine', he said, referring to the stove.

They were both tired, but each sensed a need in the other. John had a nag in his brain he had moved too fast, too soon. It was mostly the feeling that more was demanded of him, and for him to furnish leadership.

Yeah, he thought, they are truly a team now, and Suzie's upbringing was male dominated. He knew that came mostly from her Christian background, but she had turned to her father for guidance at a young age. He must do everything right, were his thoughts.

Suzie, on the other hand, wanted John to feel at ease toward her. She was aware of the limitations on personal contacts between them, but she knew it might come down to the fact she might be the control factor these next several days.

John might hold back too much. Then, again, he could lose his cool. In either case, it could very well come down to her having to set the pace. She did not believe, however, there was anything to worry about. John had shown a restraining nature, rather than one subject to questionable behavior. But, she knew this night was very important to them both, and she vowed to do her best.

Suzie reached out to grasp John's hand. She felt the need to comfort her young man. What a difference a few days can make, she thought. Now she was assuming the role of comforter, whereas before, she was the needy one. Well, maybe it hasn't changed that much, were her thoughts.

I still crave so much from John, she thought. Suzie was carried back in memory to her strong father, and how her life truly revolved around him. She realized the emotions emulating from those experiences with him, were being relived in her love and admiration for John.

'I need you in so many ways, John. And I know you need me. I have asked the Lord for his blessings on us, His children. But it will be left to you and me, through our actions, to receive those blessings', she said.

John returned the grip on his hand. He looked directly into her eyes, and kissed her. 'That is for being so mature, my love', he said.

You know I worry we may be moving too fast, but everything you say and react to, shows a maturity on your part way beyond your age. We are lucky for this weather. It is giving us precious time together that we really need', he said. 'Don't worry, sweet one. We are on the right path, and we will remain just fine'. 'Let's get in bed, and continue our conversation. I have some things to discuss with you, and cuddled up close makes it easier to hear against this wind', he said. He did not have to mention the other benefits, because Suzie's grin was speaking volumes.

The little devil he thought.

CHAPTER 54

*T*hey settled down in their cozy shelter from the cold; warm and content. John decided to just lie here awhile, as Suzie had closed her eyes. Her breathing was slow and easy, indications of a sleepy young lady. He was so pleased the way events were unfolding between them. He had worried his marriage proposal might change her attitude toward him. A young woman might reason she was obligated to be more available to her fiancée, or that some new moral criteria were in play in their relationship. How happy it made him feel, knowing Suzie was content to wait for intimacy between them.

She was asleep. There was not enough light for him to see her very well, so he put his face against hers - and went to sleep.

CHAPTER 55

*H*e came awake from the roar of the wind. Could it get any worse, he thought, as he moved to add fuel to the fire. It was colder, John could tell. This is probably the storm of the century, were his thoughts. He had calculated how long their logs and food would last, and decided they were in good shape. He had brought everything he could find from the forward galley of the plane.

They had plenty of snacks, peanuts, can drinks, and the venison. No need to worry, and the extra time they would have together meant a lot of planning for their future. Satisfied, he settled back next to Suzie.

The movement brought her awake, with a start. Panic seized her, until she felt John near.

'I was dreaming, John, and we were on a big ship together on our honeymoon. It was so real. I have hardly ever dreamed before I met you. Now, it seems I do so a lot', she said.

'I got up to tend to the fire. The blizzard has gotten stronger and it is really cold', John said. 'It is still in the middle of the night, so let's finish our sleep; okay, sweetheart?

'Oh, I do like for you to say things like that to me, John. Now, I'll really dream of you! Goodnight, sweet prince. Happy dreams to you', she said.

CHAPTER 56

Day four broke with the wind still howling, and the snow was blown side - ways. John took logs in the stove, filled the buckets with snow, and put them close to the fire, to melt. Suzie stirred.

She was completely buried in the sleeping-bag with only her face visible. She didn't want to get up. She was not tired or sleepy. Just warm and comfortable. And she was pleased about the weather. No one coming today, she thought.

John brought her a steaming mug of cocoa, along with his coffee. He slipped in the bag beside her. It was a little awkward, but they managed to drink their toddies without spilling them all over the place.

'I'll bet the storm has forced the search for this plane to be cancelled. My guesses about us being off-course, and further away from where they last heard anything, means they probably have very little knowledge of our location', he said.

'You know, Suzie, the longer it takes to find us, the more interest will have been generated by the time we are found. A young couple stranded alone for a long period of time, survivors of a crash and the worst storm ever, maybe'.

'Boy, what a story. We will be questioned relentlessly. And about every minute we were together. Suzie, I am going to tell you how I plan to handle all those inquiries. I want you to decide for yourself how you will deal with the situation', he said.

'First, I will answer all questions regarding the crash, and our survival. I am not going to talk about or answer any questions pertaining to anything about you and I. Not one answer, and if the media persists, I will walk away. There is a reason why I will do that. One question will be followed by another, and then a hundred more. Each becoming more personal', John said.

'So, I won't let that frenzy begin, Suzie', he said. 'I strongly advise you to do the same, but you make that call, you good-looking thing', he grinned. 'Your mother will blow a gasket, when she hears that, but after her first reaction, will come the thought that you and I are hiding something', he said.

Now, what could that be? None other but that John Stevens has molested her darling teen-aged daughter. Arrest that child-molester! Hang him, she would cry.

Any adult male who would abuse a juvenile, should be hanged', she will demand.

'Later, when those exact charges are brought against her husband, her very words will be used against them both', John said. 'Suzie, I'm using a lot of melodrama in describing this because I got a hunch that it is what it will be- melodrama. Now, you ponder on how you want to handle all those in-depth personal questions', he said, 'while I get everything ready for our morning snack. Afterwards, your bath will be coming up. Just in case, we get saved today', he said.

'I am so glad you are not going to answer questions about us, John. I wondered how to handle our engagement. I am proud of our commitment, but a lot of people would think we have acted in haste. I will follow your lead on that', she said.

'It is essential we talk of all these issues concerning both of us. We are going to be separated as soon as our rescuers can do so. Especially if your mother accuses me of molestation. Our only hope of staying together is for you to demand your attorney be at your side, at all times. Since you are a minor, I'm not sure they will abide by your request, but we have to try, and insist very strongly. And with a few tears. That would give them something to think about.

As a last resort, you can accuse your parents, at this time, and recite what they did to you. You can even declare that you fear for your life. Use it as a last effort, Suzie', he said. 'All hell will break loose if it gets to those last measures, as the news would spread like wild-fire. We'll discuss this later. Right now, let's eat', he said.

CHAPTER 57

*J*ohn put their food on a tray, and they had their meal. 'I am going to chop a few logs down to size. 'We have plenty, but I need to be safe', John said, as he cleared everything away and brought the steward's buggy with all the bath essentials. He got her suit case, and the box of new long-johns that remained.

'Okay, you are ready. The water is nice and warm, and you have a couple towels and wash cloths. See you later, alligator', he said.

Suzie did not linger over her bath. It was so cold. It was refreshing, though. And she wanted to be as feminine as possible. With so many layers of clothes, it was hard to detect anything which identified her as a woman, except her pretty face. She figured that was an asset. These close quarters, and 24/7 togetherness was almost too much to handle, she thought.

It worried her about any show of affection on her part might be more than John could cope with. She had so little experience to help her understand just what to say and do pertaining to their relationship. She may not know about how to read and interpret John's emotions, but hers was a different story. She felt every desire, because they were hers. She knew everything was on the brink, and it kept her in a turmoil. Prayer was her one strong ally, and it made all things right.

Almost all her prayers pertained to the relationship between John and herself. She had to make sure all was right.

CHAPTER 58

*J*ohn finished bathing, and moved everything back in the galley. 'Let's sit together in the seats next to the fire', John said.

He had added fuel to the stove and they could feel the heat. But, it was no match for the frigid cold coming from the outside.

'I would not be surprised the temperature is below minus 30 degrees. We would be frozen stiff in just a few hours, without the protections we have against that kind of weather. That would make the wind-chill factor in the -40 range.

John brought out the journal he was keeping, and began writing. 'This is our fourth day, and with these conditions, I don't believe there is any searching going on out there. It looks as if we have a few more days to spend together- alone, separated from civilization, but not desperate', he said.

'Darling, can you believe it was only a few days ago that we met? When I first saw that beautiful creature on this plane, little did I know she would steal my heart, and overwhelm my very being. All I can say be kind, sweet lady, I'm all yours', he declared.

They spent a few minutes just luxuriating in their closeness, content in each other's love. Careful not to overdo, but urgency was ever present. It was not the safest place they could be, and ever present was this storm trying to tear apart their shelter, and their lives.

These few square feet of space did give them a feeling of closeness and comfort that helped keep the fear down. But for their faith in God, and in each other, that feeling could overwhelm their better judgements.

'I saw a movie about a couple who survived a plane crash for over 40 days. The man spoke of imagining the girl as his daughter to avoid any contact initiating from him', he said. 'He had to be an older person. I could never think of you as a daughter', he said.

'I remember seeing that. At the time, I thought that sure was a long time to be lost', Suzie said. 'I never thought I would ever be in such a predicament, but here I am, happy as can be, hoping rescue is just a few days away. I think over a month would really panic me, though', she said. 'Maybe a week would be fine. In any case, we are alive and unhurt, and we are in God's hands', Suzie spoke as she held John's hands.

'We are doing so well together', John spoke in her ear. 'Very few are going to believe we retained our Christian values through all this turmoil and strife. If your mother reacts as I predict, the media will be in a frenzy. Our survival will be a huge story all by itself. Add her accusations, and we are going to see a circus.

After we announce that we will not discuss anything about our personal behavior during our ordeal, everything will truly go crazy. I have no idea how our rescue will be handled. I do feel they will want to separate us immediately, and this is what we must really fight. Probably the military will be in charge of the effort. I sure hope so. They could keep matters like the press and your mother under control', John said.

CHAPTER 59

'What do you think of offering your folks a deal. You won't file charges against them, in exchange for your mother surrendering all parental rights, and a fair share of your father's estate', he said.

'That would be fine, John, but my mother is not one to give in, if she feels there is any chance of her being right about our behavior', she said.

'Okay, so I'll call my law school professor at once. He can engage an attorney for us at home, to start legal actions on your behalf. He can also put us in touch with a lawyer up here. A local guy is a necessity, as he would know everyone we will be dealing with', John said.

'Maybe this a lot over nothing, we could get lucky one more time'. John pulled Suzie close. 'My luck has sure been good so far, young lady. Look what I have found', he said.

'Alright then, we will plan for the worse. Suzie, you will be the center of attraction, and for more reasons than one. Every person looking at your image on television, will want to see it all. The fact you are a teen-age beauty will guarantee full coverage. Add our circumstances together, along with the crash, and your mother, and the media will hound you. Also, you will have whole bunches of admirers, and some scam attempts. You will be bombarded with questions of all types', he said.

'But, most of all, men of all ages will pursue you. Not chase you down kind of 'pursuit', but by asking for dates, and even marriage proposals'.

'Oh, John, you are not serious', she said.

'Be prepared, cutie. The wolves are coming for you' he said.

Suzie had listened intently to John's words. How am I going to handle my part in this matter concerning the personal history between them. I am not good enough to completely hide my feelings. I am a poor liar, she told herself, so I won't discuss any of my emotions regarding- my fiancée! How can I not tell the world of my love, she thought. 'John, do we say anything about our love?', Suzie asked.

'Well, it would be impossible for us to both fall in love without close interaction between you and me. Then, the question would be - how close, and what did we really do. We can't keep silent about our time together and speak of love', he said. 'What do you want to do, Suzie?. I am not going to answer any question, nor will I volunteer anything. They will find out later when we have all this mess behind us. This might be a real tough aspect of this whole adventure we have to deal with. I just want to keep our personal interplay low, low key, Suzie. It will only be for a short, in any case. The media will pound us. I don't want to give them anything else to feed on', he said.

CHAPTER 60

While They relaxed before the fire, with hot beverages and little snacks, not too far away, the army unit that had been assigned to locate the presumptive crash of a commercial airplane in this vicinity, had drawn blanks for four days. Numerous rescue sorties had found nothing. The worst blizzard ever recorded in this region, was making the task almost impossible. On top of that was the fact all communications were lost with the plane, with no prior warning. No distress signals had been sent, and their transponder went dead, and they vanish from radar contact.

The commander of the search team, General Simpson was on the phone. 'Mr. President, we are doing everything we can to find the missing plane. Our search started where the aircraft was, when contact was lost. To be honest, Sir, after this length of time, and this storm raging, and the rugged terrain we are searching, I can't imagine there are any survivors', he said.

'Yes sir, we are aware of the clamor for answers. We are widening the search area, but until this storm abates, we are limited. Yes sir, we concur something knocked out everything at once.'

'They could have crashed into a mountain, or gone straight down. Or they could have flown a long time after we lost them. We are on the job, sir', he said, as he hung up.

CHAPTER 61

A media conference was waiting for him. This simple assignment seemed to be getting out of hand, he thought, as he entered the room. 'The number of attendees has increased', he addressed his aide. 'Yes sir, and they are clamoring', he answered.

'I just got a call from the president, and you can easily imagine what our conversation sounded like', he began. 'There is nothing new for us to give you. Let me say, I am surprised at how many of you people have showed up this morning. This is really bad weather for us here, and much more-so for our units in the search teams. We are out there looking, but it is rough going. I'll answer questions now', he said.

'Explain to us again what a transponder is', asked a lady reporter.

'Okay, a transponder is a radar signal constantly being sent from an airplane. It transmits data identifying the craft. Ground - control will pick this up, and can pin-point the exact location of the sender. We lost their transmission, and did not receive any radio signal thereafter. Those instruments were either turned off, or were knocked out. That could be from a crash of the plane, or a complete failure of the equipment, or a loss of power throughout the plane. The pilot could have lost all controls, or enough to prevent him from maneuvering the plane. It could have flown many miles on a straight course, in any direction. That is what we think happened, since we have no crash-scene anywhere near the location of the plane was, when last heard from', he said.

'Since we lost radar contact, the plane had to be flying at a low altitude. Which brings in the possibility of hi-jack. We discount that, unless it was deliberately destroyed. We will know that when we find the aircraft. Our search-area is very large, and this storm is killing us. It is all very rough terrain, with zero visibility. When the tempest blows over, It should not take long', he said.

CHAPTER 62

'We have a theory, as to what could have happened. Along with the loss of all controls, the pilot would be limited to the things he could do. He could possibly put the plane in a slow descent. If the plane got deep into the storm, contact could have been lost, or if it turned toward where the storm was going, i.e., about 90 degrees to the east, and was descending, then it could have been masked from the ground radar', he said.

'We have been plotting that course. However, if this had happened, then the plane would have gone down, where the storm would come right over that spot, and the storm may still be there. I believe this is what occurred, and our main focus is along that line. We must wait the storm out', the Officer said.

'We should know pretty soon now. The forecast is a couple more days of what we have now. Remember, that plane could have traveled over a hundred miles after we lost it on radar. That is a lot of territory to cover, so be patience, folks. If we felt there was any chance of survivors, we would do just what we are doing, namely, full effort. But we can't foresee anyone living through both the crash and this storm. It is sad, is it not?' he said.

CHAPTER 63

*J*ohn and Suzie knew people were looking for them. Well, not just them, but the plane. Little did the world know of their existence at this moment. Maybe no one else was aware of this small piece of real estate, but it was heaven on earth to them, and Suzie began to tear up, thinking of leaving it. She wanted to be rescued, but she loved every inch of this place. The stove, the wall that was keeping out the tempest, their seats in front of the fire, and their 'bed'.

She would never forget one moment of their time here, but way ahead of everything, was the moment John lay her on that pile of cushions, covered her with his body- and she fell in love. What will they do with our 'home', she thought.

'I was going to suggest we bathe off, and change our clothes, but maybe it would be better to put off doing that another day. We want to be real natty when we are found. This storm has abated some, but it is snowing harder. Let's eat, shall we?', he said.

John had noticed the tears in Suzie's eyes, and would have sought to comfort her. Her countenance and body language did not show any stress, so he watched closely, in case things changed. He was learning about this young beauty. He marveled at her maturity, but knew she was still a teen-ager in many ways, and John knew that was one of the reasons he loved her. His dad had spoken to him about most people being either givers or takers in their relations with other folks.

He had practiced trying to guess this trait in people's actions. He felt that training had made him the top student in his law class. Professor Hamilton commented on that fact. 'You must know what your adversary is thinking', the professor would say. 'You seem to be pretty good at making such a judgement, John', he said. He had placed himself in the middle, with some leaning toward being a giver.

Suzie was definitely a giver. He wondered about the adage, that opposites attract. We'll see, he thought, as again his mind was focusing on how much Suzie reminded him of his little sister. Same body-build, hair, and her smile! How he loved it.

CHAPTER 64

*T*hey finished their meal, and were sipping hot beverages, snuggled together in their bags. The fire was nice and warm, and both felt a touch of sleep coming on. Putting the cups aside, they soon nodded in slumber. It was the sleep of the young and innocent. Not a long nap, but very refreshing, John thought as he awoke. How much longer do we have in this cozy nook. Maybe a couple days, at the most. Then would begin the true test. We'll make it just fine, he thought.

Everything hinges on when this storm ends, as he looked at Suzie, peacefully dozing.

As if she could read his mind, that beautiful smile appeared on her face. 'I am becoming so atoned to you, I felt your eyes on me', she said. 'I was dreaming about us. You were just a few feet away, but I was unable to reach you. I could not get closer, though I tried so hard. I was in a panic. Then you smiled at me and it became ok. Your eyes did the trick. Come closer, please', she whispered.

A wave of emotions overwhelmed him. He had never felt this way before in his whole life. His desire for this lovely creature was beyond words. He could not afford to trust himself, if he embraced her.

'Suzie, I am going to be honest with you. I am not ashamed to tell you, that right now, I want you so badly, it hurts. Give me a few minutes to get control of myself', he pleaded.

'John, this is the first time you have indicated a desire for me. Believe me, I know how you feel, because I want you', she said. 'That is when I pray, John. Give me your hands, and we will ask the Lord to keep us steady and true, both to Him, and each other', she said.

Their relief was evident in the looks on each other's countenance. They knew it was going to take a lot of will-power, love, and faith from now on, for this strong emotional attraction, as natural as them breathing, had come forward in their lives. Before, it lie below the surface, now it glared at them, through their eyes. Someone said, the eyes were a mirror to one's soul, John thought. How true, how very true. 'My soul answers back- patience, dear love, patience', he said aloud.

Suzie did not know exactly why he uttered those words, but she said- 'Amen'.

CHAPTER 65

John busied himself with his journal. He recorded that the wind was not as strong, but it was snowing harder. He guessed the temperature was about the same. If they were now in the back end of the storm, the wind should change direction. He had better check on that, he thought. It could indicate the weather may clear soon.

'I'm going to open the door to the outside, Suzie. I need to monitor the direction of the wind', he said. 'That will tell us about the progress of the blizzard. A change in its speed, and which way it's blowing, lets us know something of how much longer we will have it', he said.

John opened the door, and was surprised no snow had built up outside of it. There was plenty on the ground, though. It took only a moment to gauge the wind, and John came back in, closing the door.

'The wind has swung toward the south. That would mean we are in the rear-end of the storm', he said. 'My guess is maybe one or two days of snow, then it should clear. It's just a guess, Suzie, but we will probably be rescued soon, my dear', he said.

There was a mixture of emotions as John and Suzie absorbed the news. They really were ready to move along with their relationship, and that would happen with the arrival of the rescue parties. Yet, there was a sadness thinking of their memories acquired in this place.

'John, I don't have even one bad thought about our time in this place. I wonder if they leave it like this, or will it be demolished. How wonderful if we could return years from now, and find it intact. Maybe on our 20-year wedding anniversary', she said.

'Hey, what an idea, Suzie. Let's make plans to do that, no matter what happens. We can hike up there, and celebrate, camped at this spot', he said.

'Oh, John, I can't imagine our future that far ahead, but I love the thought you and I could be back here, together', she said.

CHAPTER 66

*T*hey had their evening meal of venison, with crackers and snacks, along with hot cocoa for them both. The fire again began to hypnotize them. They cleaned up after eating, and prepared for the sleep they both needed.

'We might wake up to clear skies', John said. This could be our last night together. I'll be honest, Suzie. I am ready to be rescued, and get on with our future. Please don't take me wrong, princess. I love sleeping with you, but to be honest, I am scared to death of you. Now, let me tell you what I really need. Some TLC., to sooth my nerves', he said. 'All this talk before bed-time is bad for my heart'.

There was a big grin on John's face as he finished, and Suzie reacted by embracing the love-starved young man. 'You are really just a big boy, are you not?. That is just fine with me, because maybe I can raise you to continue to be afraid of me', she smiled.

It was a good night for both of them. The cold forced the need for John to keep the fire at full blast all night long.

'It is so cold, John', Suzie said. 'What does that mean?'.

'Well, that should indicate the storm, which is accompanied by a cold-front, is about to pass completely away from us. It's hard to believe it could get worse, as far as the temperature is concerned, but it seems to be the case', he said.

'We may be forced to stay bundled together for warmth. I'll get our toddies ready, while you keep those covers around you. I'll take the blankets down that we are using to enclose the stove. We won't be bathing today, that is for sure', he said.

CHAPTER 67

General Simpson was getting a lot of pressure from the president, on down the chain of command. The media wasn't too bad, though they were constantly demanding up-dates on the search and rescue efforts.

However, it seemed he was receiving more inquiries from the city where plane's flight originated from. All branches of the media were on the phone constantly, plus the mayor of the city, and the governor of the state. The general's aide commented on this after hanging up the phone.

'It was a local newspaper. The third today from the editor. I asked him why so much interest, when only two people from his city were on the flight. He finally admitted all of the pressure was coming from a mother, whose daughter was aboard. She had sent her teenager, alone, to visit relatives', he said.

'The editor said that she was on a rampage against the airline, appearing on the local TV stations, calling the governor, to demand more effort, to find her 'child'. 'The woman is going to get a lot of criticism for letting the young girl travel alone. How old is the young lady?', the general asked.

'She is 16 years old, and her name is Suzie Wells, according to the flight manifold', the aide answered. 'That is such a tragedy. I can't blame the mother's despair, but all this frenzy she is causing, probably stems a lot from her regret putting her on the plane', he said.

'Do we have an up-date on the weather forecast. Let's hope for an end to this blizzard. We need to find the wreckage; although, chances are very slim of us finding survivors', he said.

CHAPTER 68

Mr. Owens lived on the corner house up the same street from the Wells. He became acquainted with the father and daughter, because they would pass his house several times during their daily routine of running around the neighborhood. They always stopped and chatted at least once every day, and were very well liked by everyone.

He never saw the mother with the them. When she drove by, there were no greetings, and his next-door neighbor commented to him about her. She never displayed the loving, caring mother that she was now trying to portray herself. She was all over the media, talking about her missing daughter, bemoaning her apparent loss.

Mr. Owens recalled the incident with the young lady and her stepfather. He had true regrets of how he handled that occasion. He swore he would go to the police, and report everything as soon as they found the plane. And he was going to do it, whether Suzie was dead or alive. He was sick of seeing and hearing the female painting herself as the good parent, when her actions showed her to be something else.

One other person had boarded the ill-fated airplane at the same time as Suzie. A local football star and recent Law school graduate was being high-lighted in the media. His friend, Professor Hamilton, along with his student, John Stevens, were mentioned on the tv today. Mr. Owens made a note to call the man, for legal advice about how he should proceed against Suzie's mother.

CHAPTER 69

*J*ohn and Suzie were fast asleep. The extra blankets had made it
real comfortable, as long as no part of the body was exposed to
the outside. They had a few days experience by now, so emotions were
calm and collected. Their nightly ritual of joint prayer, however, was
the singular act they both agreed which gave them peace, and was the
glue cementing their relationship.

The night passed quietly, except John getting up to replenish the
fire. They needed the warmth it furnished, and the blaze gave them
a sense of safety, even though they were sleeping. How primitive was
this, John thought. Man providing food and shelter for his mate, and
protecting against all evil spirits, and demons. Stuff like that inspired
epic movies, he thought. And went back to sleep.

CHAPTER 70

*T*heir sixth day started as the others had. They had something to eat and a mug each of a hot drink. This morning, John had coffee, and Suzie had hot chocolate, but instead of getting up, they burrowed into the covers. 'It is really cold', John said. 'And I sound like a broken record. But, baby, it is cold outside,' he said.

Suzie began to sing - Let it snow, let it snow, etc. All of this was to ease the tension they both felt mounting, as the time was surely approaching when they would be rescued. It wasn't the act of being found, so much as the uncertainty of what would happen next. They both felt the need of prayer. Holding hands, they knelt together. And peace and tranquility were their reward. 'I think I know why the Lord answers our needs. We are truly His children, with open hearts, and devoid of deceit', he said.

A song from his church days came to his mind. 'Burdens were lifted at Calvary, Jesus is very near'. How true; really-How true. They had an awful lot to be thankful for, both thought, as they finished the beverages. 'It is too cold to fully bathe. We can sponge it, and change into fresh duds, We have one full change apiece left. That should last the rest of the way', John said.

CHAPTER 71

*P*rofessor Hamilton answered his phone. An old friend, Bill Owns was on the line.

'Professor, you were on the TV station yesterday, talking about your law student, missing along with the young lady from here. I have something very important to talk to you about her. Her father was a fairly good friend of mine. He died several years ago', he said, and began telling the professor of his encounter with the girl and her mother.

'I made a big mistake letting them talk me out of calling the authorities. Will you advise me of my best course of actions, as I want to bring this forward', he said. 'I do want to say my next-door neighbor, Mr. Alan Johnson, saw the whole encounter, but was not close enough to hear anything. He did notice the torn blouse on Suzie, and her disarray at the time. I did not tell him what had occurred, much to my regret, until yesterday. He had seen the events on the media, and had remembered what had happened before. He really read me the riot-act for how I handled the whole thing', he said.

'I believe Suzie was put on that plane, to get her away from here as fast as possible, because of what her stepfather did to her', he said.

'What we do about this, Mr. Owens, depends on the outcome of this plane crash. If there are no survivors, then we take everything to the authorities. Now, you may think I am senile, but I still hold out hope that my student, John Stevens, is alive. And if he is, then Suzie could be also. That is why we must wait until we know, for sure', he said.

'My reasoning on this matter stems from my confidence in John. If there is a way, he will have found it, and he would bring Suzie through it, too. I don't think they know each other, but I have been shown the seating arrangement on the plane, and those two were alone toward the rear of the plane. He would save that girl, if he could. We will know, for sure, shortly, I think'.

'In the meantime, I want to get a deposition from you, and from Mr. Johnson. Don't talk to anyone at all about this, Mr. Owens. That includes everyone, especially the Sloan family. The odds are against our young friends, but we must wait. The Sloans will be complacent, and we are going to nail them', he said.

CHAPTER 72

The day was being spent in their sleeping-bags, with blankets wrapped close. It took some time to warm up after they bathed and changed. Suzie felt she would never get warm, but a snuggle and some hot chocolate saved her life, and soon she was smiling again. 'Do you notice the wind is not blowing as hard', he asked. 'It depends on where they are searching as to how long we have here. Suzie, did it occur to you the way I spoke to you just then?. I spoke of when we will be found, not if. I don't want for us to be worried about our future, neither the 'near' or the 'distant'. Everything will work out just fine', he said.

'Make sure you keep insisting that you need your attorney with you at all times. We need to stay together. If we are separated, clam up completely. Keep repeating- I want my lawyer', he said.

CHAPTER 73

'The weather reports were showing the storm had drifted quite a bit in the past few hours. We are bringing in the search-teams right behind the movement. Everything points to the plane crashing along the storm's path, since we haven't found it anywhere else', General Simpson said.

'Captain Baker, I'm putting you in charge of Team-A. You will lead the search in this area', he said as he pointed at a spot on the map. 'It is extremely rugged terrain, as you can see. I don't have to tell you how to do your job. You are the best I have, so - good hunting', he said, as he returned the captain's salute.

Captain Baker addressed his command. 'At 0500 hours in the morning, we will begin our search patterns. Get a good night's sleep. We intend to fly all day, if necessary. Let's find those people', he said.

'Our base will be a long way from our search, so we will have to return for fuel frequently. Which means our efforts must be thorough and accurate. I will be in the com-center, so be sure to keep us informed of your positions. Keep the channels open. There will be no chit-chat, because we will be monitored', he said.

CHAPTER 74

*J*ohn could not see how any search other than helicopter would be possible, because of the snow. The wind was mostly gone, only a slight breeze remained.

'I don't think we will be getting up any time soon. It is really cold. But, I have been saying that for a few days, haven't I, dear lady. I would go outside again, but I can't imagine what I would see, other than the snow fall. So, you stay warm, and I'll bring our lunch, and warm up our toddies', he said.

After finishing their meal, John began to bring his journal up to date. Suzie sat close to him, both for warmth, and for love. It all was so calm and serene, and peaceful. Her eyes suddenly became very droopy, and her head nodded. John felt her body relax, as she fell asleep. He put his arm around her shoulders, and cradled her warmly. It was just a few minutes later when he began doing the same thing. He lowered them both, and together they slept the sleep of innocence.

CHAPTER 75

Suzie came awake first, slightly unsure of her circumstances. Then, she remembered everything when she saw John, still asleep beside her. Her movements brought the man from his sleep.

'I guess we were tired. This cold does seem to sap a person of energy. We didn't nap very long, because the fire is still pretty strong', he said.

'I really needed the rest', Suzie said. 'But, right now I need some TLC, young man. Not a whole lot, just a few hugs will do. You got any you can loan me?', she whispered. 'I will need to store them for the future, in case you are not close by later on'.

John could tell that she was a little anxious. They were getting closer to being rescued, and the uncertainty of everything bothered her more than it affected him.

'Don't you fret, sweetheart. We may have setbacks, but as long as we stay on the straight and narrow, there will be a warm ending. I emphasize the 'warm', he said. I know I sound really corny, Suzie. You can say this suspense of waiting for things to happen is driving me crazy, and you could very well be on target. I'll be alright, though, because 'I've got my love to keep me warm', John said.

'John, I suspect you are trying to take my mind off the worries I have. Thank you, for being so kind, but put your arms around me right now. I am cold, a little sad, and in love, so come here', she said.

'Okay, but let's have a word of prayer together. My whole outlook on everything becomes so different after I thank the Lord. I want you to know I get such a joy, holding your hands, and praying with you', he said. It was much easier to hold each other after remembering God in their lives.

They lay close, bundled against the frigid weather, content, and happy. Sleep would have engulfed them, if John had not noticed the sun shine coming through the window by the stove.

'Holy cow', he exclaimed. 'Suzie, the storm has passed. Look at the sunlight', he said. 'I'm going outside for a moment. Let's get our parkas on and look around'.

CHAPTER 76

*T*here was at least two feet of snow down the slope, and even more below. The sky was clear, and they could see the mountains in the distance. 'That means we will be found shortly, Suzie', the man said.

He turned to face her, as he held her tight. He felt the mixed emotions she was having. This little oasis in the middle of the desert would always be a safe haven for them. Far from being a wreckage, the site of tragedy for others, everything about this place was a refuge they would forever remember.

'I have a piece of metal covering the logs I gathered for a bonfire. I'll wait until morning before clearing it off. We need to shovel a path down to the clearing below. It will show anyone flying over that someone is alive here, and we don't want people tracking snow into our 'home'. I hope they are far away right now. Tomorrow will be soon enough for us to be saved. Don't want them to spoil our last night here-together', he said.

'John, you foresaw the plane crash. You got it right about the storm and you have prepared me for this rescue. I not only love you, but think you are the smartest man alive. This may be our last night, for a-while, or maybe ever. I am going to savor it, John. And it will be another wonderful event we will look back on. I trust the Lord is watching over us right now. Let's get to bed, and we will offer up our prayer of thanksgiving-together', Suzie said.

I am going to enjoy this night, she thought. No rush to go to sleep, as she held John in her arms. With so many layers of clothes, and sleeping-bags between them, he was just a bundle she was holding.

His breath on her neck was another thing, however. It was their connection to each other.

She knew that he was awake, but they did not speak. She marveled at the serenity of their embrace. Both these young lovers knew that future events might be beyond their control, but they, together, would prevail. Soon, the even breathes of slumber arose from each of them, and all was well!

CHAPTER 77

*I*t was still when they got up. Well, really John was the only one 'up'. Suzie lie snug, watching her 'man' prepare their beverages, stoke the fire, and return beside her.

'I'll clear the area and light the bonfire in a couple hours', he said. 'I want to lie here a little longer', Suzie said. 'The drinks can wait. Come back and get me warm', she said. They snuggled for over an hour. 'Couldn't they find us without the bonfire', Suzie asked.

'They probably can. It would make it easier. It's rough terrain around us. But we will forego the fire for now. Tell you what. If we hear a plane, then we will light it', he said.

'Okay. I want some more time with you. Now that rescue is imminent, I want to put it off', she said.

If the rescue party had arrived just now, they would have found two kids, laughing their heads off. Suzie had got up to get the drinks, and had asked John- 'What will it be. Coffee, tea, or me, and John burst out laughing, as he answered - 'me'. That set Suzie off, too. They snuggled under the covers, drifting into sleep.

CHAPTER 78

*T*hey were unaware when the plane had found the wreckage. 'This is Tango-3, to base', the pilot radioed. I have picked up a signal that could be the plane's black-box. It is faint and dead ahead. I'll stay on the air while I approach. I have never seen rougher country. With the snow cover, the wreak may not be visible. The signal is getting stronger, so I'm on the right course, he said.

John came awake. He had heard the aircraft. He sprang up, and began to dress. 'What's wrong, Suzie asked.

'A plane is near. I need to light the bonfire', he replied, as he opened the door. He quickly pulled the metal away, and poured the fuel he had stashed, on the pile, and lit it. The fire blazed up, just as the plane came over the mountain in front of them.

'Tango 3 to base. Someone just lit a big fire down in the valley. We have at least one survivor. Yes, I can make out a tail section, and it is intact, forward about ten or twelve feet of where the engines would be mounted. I can make out one person. No, another survivor has emerged. We have two people so far. I have to turn and make another pass. I'll come in as low as possible, he said.

'I can see the two clearly, now. It looks like one male, and one female. Wait a minute. The guy is holding a piece of metal. Looks like he spelled out in black tape-Two-unhurt. There is a clear area in front of the tail, and the guy was clearing it of snow as I turned. Smart to let us know about their condition. We won't need medical stuff right away', he reported.

'At least three copters could land where he was working. How did those two survive the blizzard; not to mention the plane crash. Over, I'm coming in', the pilot said.

'Wait a sec. The guy is holding another sign, with two names. J. Stevens and S. Wells, it reads. Good job, fellow', he says, as he wags his wings, and turns away, headed home.

CHAPTER 79

*J*ohn continued clearing the snow for the next arrivals. 'They may be a long way off. Could be as much as one hundred miles to their base of operations', he said. 'We gave them enough information to ease any need to employ break-neck speed to get a lot of people here, so I would guess it will be several hours before they get folks on the ground with us. Let's go inside and rearrange things to hide how we actually slept. No need to give them any ideas about us. We'll have our breakfast in the seats by the fire, and that will establish our second sleeping area', he said.

'How many people do you think will be coming?', she asked.

'No telling, honey'. He stopped talking, as Suzie's eyes widened, as if she were in shock.

'You called me 'honey', she cried, as she bounded toward him, arms out wide. It is the first time, and how wonderful you sounded. John, I truly needed your little word of endearment. I am scared. I just know they will separate us', she said.

John held her, as he attempted to console the young lady. 'Remember to demand the presence of your attorney. Make a big scene. Refuse to move, or be moved.

And, above all, don't talk to anyone. Now, Suzie, They may not try anything like we talked over. Stay calm; look pretty, young, and defenseless, in any case. You may not fully understand just how powerful a person you are, but I want to say you pack a big wallop', he exclaimed. 'It is your looks, your age, and you're a female. With those assets used the right way, anyone would be a fool to mess with you. At least at first, so be firm', he said.

'It all depends on how your mother reacts. We don't have a lot of control, except over things right here, so it remains with us to make a strong effort, on our part. I am going to insist we be allowed to stay together, also. Have faith, dear lady', he said.

CHAPTER 80

*A*fter Professor Hamilton finished his conversation with Bill Owens, he placed a call to a former pupil at the law school. Sam Brown lived in the area where the missing airliner was last heard from. 'Good to hear from you, sir', Mr. brown said as he answered the phone. 'I have been keeping up with the search for that plane, because you indicated when we set up the job interview, the young man in question was on his way up here. I figured he would be aboard', he said.

'You are correct, Sam. John Stevens was on the plane. I told you about his family, so I am the only person, except his elderly grandmother, that he has left to act in his behalf. I have received her permission to act as John's attorney. I don't have any legal standings right now, but I have petitioned the court here, to be named his executor, in the event he died in that plane. If and when that is enacted, I want you act as his attorney up there.

'There is a second matter, regarding another passenger on the plane. A young teen-ager, Miss Suzie Wells, was aboard. I'll send you an email giving you full details concerning her. It is truly a bizarre story. I hope those two young people are alive, but in case they are dead, I will need your expertise, Sam', he said.

'Thank you for asking, sir, and I accept the job, with relish. I will call the Governor, whom I know quite well, and get him to arrange for me to be allowed at the command - post of the search effort. I'll keep you informed of the efforts to find the plane', he said, as he terminated the telephone call.

CHAPTER 81

Captain Baker was standing at the podium, in front of a packed room full of media people that had come from all over the world. The command center had announced the press conference would have news about the missing airplane.

Sam Brown had received the call from the governor's office about the conference and just made it on time, as the captain began.

'We have some very good news, and some bad news, too. The wreckage of flight 078 has been located. The site is 76 miles from here, in this mountain range'. He was pointing at a large map on the screen behind the podium.

'The good news is that there are two survivors. A man and woman greeted our plane as it circled overhead. They wrote their names on a piece of material. The man is John Stevens, and the female is Suzie Wells. The only other information we got, was that they were not injured' he said.

'The tail section of the plane is intact, and it looks like they took refuge in it. We have another plane headed back there now, and we'll have answers as to how they lived through the blizzard' he said.

Sam Brown went outside and called Professor Hamilton. 'They found the plane, sir, and our two friends are the only ones alive', he said.

'The television station had the conference on the air, and I saw it', the professor said. 'The station is attempting to contact Suzie's mother. I am going to be watching this closely. Get back in the conference, and introduce yourself', he said.

'Tell the captain you have been retained as John's attorney. If he questions you, tell him Mr. Stevens' grandmother has hired you. I have cleared this with her. I expect an adverse reaction from Suzie's mother, so be prepared to include the young lady as a client later. You got my email concerning Suzie, so you know about her problems. I'll be in touch', he said.

CHAPTER 82

'I don't know what will happen next, but I suspect another plane before long. Maybe you should go inside to keep warm', John said.

'No, I'll stay here with you. I'm fine with this heavy coat. I hope the owner doesn't mind me wearing it' Suzie said.

She was nervous, and her glib comment showed her feelings. Her reaction to John's 'honey' remark eased the tension building in her, as was his response. 'The wait isn't doing me any good, either', she said.

John looked at her, trying to make sense of her conversation. 'Take it easy, young lady. All will end well', he said.

'We depend on each other, so don't hold back if you need anything. We are an 'item', my dear. A very special one. Forged in the fires of battle, annealed by the Lamb of God, and nurtured in our love. The world beware! Here we come, ready or not', he exclaimed with passion.

All of that was too much for Suzie. She fell into his arms, weeping. They were in this embrace, when they heard the plane approach them. 'We will take up this position later, honey, and don't you forget it', he cooed.

CHAPTER 83

*T*he plane came right at them, and dropped a package that parachuted close by. John retrieved it. He opened to find they had sent a two-way radio set. He followed instructions and got it ready to use. 'This is John S. calling', he said. 'Over'.

'I hear you, loud and clear. This is Major Smith, from NORAD. How are you doing. Over', he said.

'We are fine. We have plenty of food, and are completely enclosed in the tail section of the plane. We also have a roaring fire in the stove we built. Over', John said.

'Major Smith here. I heard you correctly, did I not, say you built a stove. Over'.

'Yep', John said. 'And we found sleeping-bags, blankets, and a box of long-johns in the cargo container, so we are quite snug. Over', he ended.

'You obviously survived the crash unhurt. Everyone is wondering how you managed to do it, but seeing the part of the plane you are in, you were able to get to it, before the plane went down.

Over', the major said.

'We will give you the whole story later. How long before people arrive here, is our real concern. Over', John said.

'It will be tomorrow. Since neither of you folks are injured, they are going to bring in three copters at once, with a full rescue crew, and some media people, too. Also, they want to gather the remains of those that did not survive as soon as possible. Over'.

'Major, this situation is bigger than you can imagine. I am a 21-year-old freshly minted attorney, single male. I have been marooned, alone, with a 16-year-old that could be 'Miss America', and I mean it literally. I'm sure you know what the media will make of our situation. Right now, I need you to answer a few questions. First, who will be in charge of this rescue mission. Second, where do you plan taking us.

Third, under whose authority will we be placed-military, state, airline, or other.

Fourth, there is an important issue pertaining to Miss Wells, which will come out in due time. I can't discuss that at this time. Fifth, do we get protection from the media frenzy coming from reporters, news organizations, television and radio coverages, and just plain thrill-seekers. Please answer in good time, because we are not leaving this place, until you do. Over', John said.

'Wow, you have spent a lot of time and thought on this matter. Over', the major said.

'Yes, we have, sir. I want you people to do the same thing. I am bringing all this up now, so we will not have surprises, and so-called big wigs telling us they have no plans for such-and such event. And you are aware where some folks will want to take this happening, do you not? We will not be a part of a circus, sir. We will refuse to leave here, or we will strike out across the wilderness by ourselves, if we have to. And one more thing. I feel certain efforts will be made to separate the two of us. We won't let this happen. Over' he said.

CHAPTER 84

'I have recorded all this, and will be back. Over and out'. 'Why was he so abrupt at the end?', Suzie asked. 'I suppose he took offense at some of my questions. He had expected two helpless, and defenseless individuals, just begging to be rescued. Instead, we are making demands from the hands who feed us', he laughed.

CHAPTER 85

'We must be totally together on our plan of operation, Suzie. Tell me how you stand on these matters, Oh High Princess. Do we face the wrath of the world, as one?', he said.

'We are together, lover', she said.

'Okay, I'll put you on the radio when the call comes in, and you can tell them I am your attorney, and Mr. Stevens is to act upon all matters, pertaining to me, both civil and criminal. Tell him anything he asks of you except you are in love, are engaged to be married, and this guy, John Stevens adores you. I added the 'criminal' part, just in case' he said.

Since they would remain in their shelter another night, John put logs on the fire, and arranged their bed. It was still very cold, though the excitement had kept them from thinking about it. They huddled together as they ate.

'John, this may be our last meal together for some time. I am so pleased you have led us in prayer before every one of our repasts. Dad always offered our thanks, though you could tell Mom just tolerated the prayer', she said.

'Oh, John, all my dreams are coming true. Everything I wished for in life, except Dad's passing, is happening to me. When he left, I thought all my future was over, especially after my mother turned on me. Now, It's even better, because of you, dear man. You know, maybe it was a god-send for those moments in my life. It made me grow up almost overnight, so to speak', she said. 'It helped prepare me for this time here with you'.

CHAPTER 86

'Come on, let's duck into those bags, and get warm. I'll put the radio next to the bed, because they are sure to call tonight', John said. No sooner said than done, as the radio-phone rang. 'Are you there', the voice asked. John noted it was the same person, which was promising.

'We are here, John said, as he keyed the set. 'This is General Simpson calling. I am the person in charge of this mission', he said. 'I have your list of questions, and I must say I find them and your attitude quite demanding. Over', he said.

'Well, General Simpson, let me remind you that neither Miss Wells, nor myself, created this so called 'mission'. We are here, alive and well because of our work and good fortune, and not through any efforts of you, the airline, or anyone associated with you. We did not endure these hardships to listen to you criticize our simple requests. So, if this is all you have to offer, we say 'goodbye'. We will talk the media. Over and out', John said.

'Hold on, Mr.' Stevens. Could I please start over? I apologize for my opening remarks. We were not prepared for demands by those who are to being rescued. I use that word figuratively, considering what you guys have done. Again, I am sorry for my approach to you. May we start over, please', he said.' 'Over'.

'Fine, General Simpson. First, I am a newly minted lawyer, but fully certified. I am going to put Miss Wells on right now, as she has something to say', he said.

'This is Suzie Wells, and I wish to make this statement. Due to circumstances I will explain at a later date, I have hired Mr. Stevens as my attorney. I do this of my own free will. I will demand my attorney be with me at all times. Any questions, sir?', she asked.

'This is John back on. We cannot discuss the reasons Miss Wells chose this course of action, on the radio. I will tell you it concerns the very serious matter of why Miss Wells was on this plane, alone, having been literally forced to do so against her wishes. Does that tell you enough, General Simpson?', he asked.

CHAPTER 87

'Yes, it does, and it somewhat explain a few of your requests. Over', he said.

'Add this to the mix, sir. An adult male, alone with a beautiful 16 year-old minor female, in close quarters together, for an extended period of time. Survivors of a plane crash, and all during one of the worse storms, I daresay, to ever hit this region. It all means Miss Wells, and I will be swamped, unless you help us. I expect there will be efforts made to separate us. That is why Miss Wells has requested that I accompany her', John said.

'We are not going to leave her alone against that horde of media and public officials, who will come at her from every angle imaginable, sir. And we expect an assault from another quarter, that we won't name at this time, so do what you can for us, and thanks', John said. 'Over'.

'Our people will come in around noon. Other planes could be flying over earlier, but they won't land. The whole area has been classified as a restricted crash site, but interest in this event is very high, and people will do anything to get a jump on the field, so to speak. In my estimation, the airline folks will give you the most trouble. They will claim jurisdiction, and might defy my off-limits order', he said. 'Over and out'.

CHAPTER 88

*S*uzie had sat quietly, listening and watching. For the first since they met, she was not the central focus of this young man. She detected an iron will in her 'man', one similar she knew her father had. It did not disturb her, she reflected. She realized their relationship was fast becoming a partnership, as well as a love affair. Platonic to a certain degree, but a love affair, in every other way. She felt comfortable waiting for him to finish his talk with the general, and come back to her.

John did not disappoint her as he turned off the radio, and grabbed her in a bear-hug. 'Do you realize it has been over an hour since you kissed me, pretty lady?'

'Well, if I kiss you two times, that will catch us up', she said.

'Then I can go for overtime', John said. They both knew this night could be their last together for some time. Thanks to the vow they had taken and the faith they shared, kisses and hugs eased the tension. John had piled a lot of logs on the bonfire and it blazed brightly, casting light into the plane.

'I like looking at you this way. I'll be asleep in a short time, with the picture of your face in my mind', she said. It was only a few minutes, and all was well. Both slept the sleep of innocence.

CHAPTER 89

While peace and tranquility reigned supreme at the crash site, that was assuredly not the case at the home of Suzie's parents. The news they just received shook them to their toes.

While neither person wanted Suzie dead, her being alive created serious problems for both of them. They immediately paid a visit to the attorney who handled Suzie's father's estate, and had been retained after the assumed plane crash. They were all ready to cash in on that event.

The lawyer had not been informed of the incident involving the stepfather and Suzie, so the parents told him their version of what happened. 'I know a lot about the guy that survived along with your daughter. He was a football star at the university, and a recent graduate of the law school there. He passed the state bar and received his certification just days before his whole family was wiped out in a car wreck', he said. Do you recall reading about it?

'Yes we do, and that is why we are here. We are sure Suzie would have told him of the occurrence concerning her stepfather. I sent Suzie on that trip right afterwards, to go live with her father's family. Her account probably differs a lot from ours, so we must discredit her, to brand her the nymphomania that she is. The male is an adult, so any sexual activity between them would put him in jail, and would prove our charge against Suzie' she said.

'I am going to start demanding that the authorities immediately begin an investigation and insist Suzie be subjected to a rape test. Evidence of any sexual activity would be detectable, and conclusive proof against them both', she said.

'The young lady does not have to consent to such an examination, especially if she denies any sexual contact between them', the lawyer stated.

'Then we go before a judge, demanding proof my daughter was not raped. If she was subjected to sexual intercourse, then it would be statutory rape. If there is nothing to hide, why the objection,

I will demand', she said. 'We can't lose'.

'Oh, yes you can', the lawyer said. They may not have been any such contact. And if it is true, and Suzie comes forth with her accusation that she was attacked, she told you of it, and you send her packing without reporting the incident, then you two will be in deep-something. Trying to frame you own daughter to protect your husband will get you both jail-time', he said.

'Whose side are you on', the mother said.

'You hired me to give legal advice and guidance, and that is what I have done. You don't like it, then I am gone', he said. 'Furthermore, Mr. Stevens graduated at the top of his class. He passed the bar exam on his first try, with some of the highest scores ever recorded. I know this because his law professor is a good friend of mine, who thinks the world of this young man. Such a mind would foresee the pitfalls of getting involved with a teen-age girl in such a close-ended situation. I find it hard to believe he would abuse your daughter', he said.

'I am sorry I spoke to you like that. We need your help', the mother said.

'Okay, here is my advice. Wait and see. We know they survived, possibly due to some heroic action by Mr. Stevens. If true, your daughter would consider him a hero. He a very handsome young man, and only a few years older. Well within her range of acceptable males; by age, looks, and success. So If she thinks she loves the guy, she will protect him, if she can', he said. 'She could very well agree to forget the incident with her stepfather in exchange for you leaving them both alone' he said.

Mrs. Sloan, Suzie's mother, listened to what her lawyer had to say. She could not make herself forget about the threat her daughter posed to her husband, nor could she believe his assessment of what happened between the young couple.

'I will never be convinced the man is innocent. He may be the finest male on earth, but if there was sexual contact between the two, then he is not innocent. Suzie is a very poor liar. She would break down under questioning pertaining to their behavior', she addressed her husband. 'I hope you are with me. I want to go after Mr. Stevens, as the only way to discredit Suzie', she said.

'Okay with me. Let's go', he said.

CHAPTER 90

Suzie was awake, watching her fiancé in sleepy, peaceful repose. She knew this would be their last day in this haven, and it would be a long and difficult one for them both. This moment of privacy would not come again any time soon. Maybe that would not be such a bad thing, she thought. Last night showed the bad side of privacy to them both. Well, not really bad, just hard to limit their contact.

Young engaged couples don't normally have to deal with such long periods of togetherness.

She thanked the Lord for his guidance, bolstering their desire to face the world without feeling any regret. She recalled the teachings of her father and the love she had for him. Their Christian faith was the extra bond between them.

And now, this new chapter in her life. Time had smoothed the rough path she traveled after his death, making it possible to cope today.

John became aware Suzie was up, when she whispered something he couldn't make out. She was next to him, obviously in deep thought. It had to be good thoughts, as her face was relaxed. She turned that beautiful face toward him.

'I was thinking of my dad', she said. 'He set a pretty high standard in my aspirations for a mate, young man. You fill the bill', she said. 'I had doubts I would ever meet a man I could say those words to. The Lord must have arranged our introduction, John. How else could such a convoluted meeting take place. What a story-book tale we have to tell our children. I can truly look forward to those days', she said.

John could only smile, as he held her hands. He knew he had a lot to live up to. Most men can start slowly, and build gradually on a relationship, but this one began so dramatically. what a reputation to maintain.

'Well, young lady, I agree with you, on the Lord's help, but most of the inspiration, or the cause of that inspiration, came from two people making you an angel; truly a beautiful adorable human being. I promise to strive diligently to uphold such faith you show in me. So mote it be', he said.

'What was it you just said?', she asked.

'That is a masonic phrase for, Amen', he said. 'Are you a mason, John? she asked. Dad was a mason, the Grand Master of his lodge'.

'Yes, I am, Suzie. I just joined last year. Professor Hamilton was my sponsor. That is one of the reasons we have close ties. I wonder if your father knew him.

Speaking of Mr. Hamilton, he has heard by now about us living through the crash. I must ask Captain Baker for a phone. We have people to contact', he said.

CHAPTER 91

*J*ohn turned the radio on, but nothing was on the air. He was glad. We need a little more time this morning, he thought. They ate and sat drinking their hot beverages.

'I expect this place will start hopping real soon', John said. 'We'll finish up here, and get everything in order. As soon as you get all prettied up, I'll take our bags to the door'. John took Suzie in his arms.

Tears had formed in her eyes, as he talked about leaving this place. 'I am ready to go, John. My tears are not from sadness, as much as remembrance of what we accomplished here. I know we will come back here in the future, and maybe have some additions tagging along with us', she cried.

'Our past is for us to recall in our minds; Our future is for us to live, together, pretty lady', he said.

They dressed, and packed their bags. John arranged the sleeping bags separately, with two on the bed, and one in the seats by the fire.

'This will show how we slept, to the outside world. We can't give them any ideas. As if we are going to influence the horde about to descend on us', John said.

'Stay close, and keep that wonderful smile on your face. I am telling you, those people are going into shock, when they see you. You have just the right amount of make-up on, to highlight your natural beauty. I hope you haven't gotten tired of me keep talking about you', he said.

'No, I have not, John, nor will I ever', she answered.

'Okay, let us enter - stage right. Only, there is no audience', he said, as they opened the door, and into bright sunshine. It was still quite cold, so John tossed a couple big logs on the bonfire, stirred the embers, and they soon had a nice fire.

At that moment, the radio came on. 'This is Captain Baker here. You read me? Over'.

'We hear you very well, captain. We just brought the fire back to life, and await your arrival', John said. 'Over'.

'We are only a little ways out. Should be about a half-hour. We have two copters with us, and one following later, loaded with the media and their gear. I wanted some time alone with you guys, so I scheduled an hour's separation'. he said. 'Over, and Out'.

'I am going to go down and clear some more snow from the landing area. The blades of the helicopters should sweep most of it away. It's very powdery, and will really get stirred up, so let's go back inside and wait by our fire', John said.

'We'll go outside when it settles down', he said.

It was hard work clearing the landing area. John had used all of the timber the crash had leveled on the bonfire and their stove, so it was only the snow to move, but there was so much. He finally gave up, and headed back.

Then he heard the distinct noise of an approaching helicopter. The sound was from the rear of the wreckage. He walked around toward the noise, just in time to see the craft land in a cloud of blown snow. On the side was the markings indicating it was a private plane. They had landed outside the crash area, in a small clearing behind him.

John noted this, because the captain had mentioned that where he was, had been declared off-limits. He felt sure these people were not part of the rescue efforts. Out jumped four men, followed by a large crate. Work began immediately on setting up some equipment next to the plane. The men made no effort to communicate with him, as they mounted several tripods. As they worked, it was evident to John, their goal was to establish a communications link to a satellite.

Two more men emerged from the copter. One was holding a microphone, the other had a large camera on his shoulder. 'Hello, young man. You must be John Stevens', the man said. 'We are here to interview you guys'.

CHAPTER 92

This was obviously an effort to be the first to broadcast from the crash, and outside the scheduled arrangements made by Captain Baker and General Simpson. John turned his back to the man, and started toward the plane section. He had no intention to talk to these people.

'Hey, Mr. Stevens, wait up and give us a chance. We were shut out of the so-called official group. They only allowed the big boys, citing space requirements as the reason we were denied' he said.

John stopped, and stood still, as he pondered the situation.

'Okay, turn your equipment off', he said. 'Put the mike down, and move away from the camera. Tell me your name', John spoke.

The man did as John had requested. 'My name is William Brady', he said.

'Mr. Brady, Suzie and I are in a very unique situation that I cannot discuss with you right now. We require the help of the people in charge of this rescue operation. If I allow you to interview us, all chances of those folks aiding our cause, is gone. I cannot afford that, Mr. Brady. I noted where you landed, and will assume you avoided the crash site, which has been put off-limits. That means you should not be forced to leave', he said.

'The rescue people will be here in just a few minutes, so I don't have enough free time for an interview right now. I will bring Suzie out, and we will pose for you, if you promise to delay airing for a couple hours', John said.

'We agree, for sure, and thanks', Bill said.

John and Suzie stood together as the camera recorded them. The interview was concluded by the arrival of two military helicopters. 'That will be all, folks, for now', John said. 'If we get a chance, we will come back to you'.

CHAPTER 93

Captain Baker spotted the civilian copter as he landed. 'What is that craft doing here', he said. He ordered his aide to go over and find out who they are. 'I noticed they landed outside the crash zone, so all we can do is warn them to stay out, if that is what you want', the aide said. 'I hope those two kids realized that plane is not part of our operation. Right now, we will proceed as planned, and deal with them later', the captain said.

John and Suzie waited outside the door for the captain and his men to climb up the hill to greet each other. 'This is Suzie Wells, and I am John Stevens. We welcome you all to our 'home', so to speak', he said.

John could tell all the men were stunned by Suzie's appearance. She had a regal look on her face, which made her both beautiful, and utterly majestic. They had not been prepared for such a woman, that was for certain, John thought.

Captain introduced everyone, immediately turned to the plane behind them. John spoke up at once. 'They landed a few minutes ago. Suzie and I went out to meet them, as they were setting up a bunch of equipment. I knew from the plane's marking that were not with your group. They were excluded from coming with the 'big' outfits. I told them we would talk after finishing with you guys. Any objections?', John asked.

'No, as long as they stay where they are, which is off this site. I am going to have enough trouble as it is. If this one can come in here, on their own, there will be others. My aide is talking to them now. We will deal with this matter later', he said.

Captain Baker indicated he wanted to enter the plane's interior, so with John and Suzie, the three walked into the place that had served as a refuge since the crash. He had looked the young folks over closely, noting their clean and neat appearances.

'I must say, you don't look like plane-crash and wild storm survivors. I see how you walled in the front, sealing it against the weather. I see your stove. I can't figure where you got the material to build it', he said.

John explained about the door retrieved from the wreckage, the wire used to hold it together from the same place, and finding other items from the cargo containers.

'This is a nice cozy place to ride out a blizzard, but it took time to do all this work. How did you do it, through such a tempest?', he asked.

John explained how he foresaw what was to befall them, and acted immediately, finishing just as the storm arrived.

All during the conversation, the captain kept his attention on the young teen-ager. He knew he would not be the first person to wonder what had transpired between these two youngsters, both mentally, and physically. He had been told of Suzie's mother and her accusations against Mr. Stevens.

'I want to tell you of a development that occurred last night. Your mother, Suzie, held a press conference, mainly to demand you be taken into custody immediately, and be given a 'rape' examination. She says she wants proof this adult male molested you, a juvenile female during the time you were alone, in this place', he said.

Much to the captain's surprise, Suzie Wells smiled at him. 'John and I expected this reaction from my mother, Captain Baker. There is much more besides this matter that motivated my own flesh-and blood to make these charges', she said. As she spoke, she had reached out for John's hand, and was now holding it.

CHAPTER 94

'As you know, Miss Wells has retained me as her attorney. We will be asking the courts to vacate Suzie's mother, Mrs. Sloan, of her parental rights. This entire matter will be enacted in a court-of-law, Captain. However, it will be a huge source of gossip, speculation, and downright prejudice until then', he said.

'I want to thank you for waiting until you were alone with us to bring this matter to our attention. This is to be the only public statement Suzie and I will make on this. During our time alone, together, Suzie and I have fallen in love with each other. When she reaches her 18th birthday, I hope and pray we will be married, or at least, be able to do so. I want Suzie to tell you the rest', he said.

'Captain Baker, I do not fear such an examination as my mother proposes, for I am a virgin. My Christian faith, the same faith John has, and our vows to each other kept us alive, Captain, and chaste', she said.

'We will not answer any questions, what so ever, pertaining to any action, or words, between Suzie Wells, and myself. I want to ask you to keep what we have told you confidential. We sensed in you a man of integrity. We need a person on our side, Captain baker. This a private matter, and we know it does not need to be reported. However, if we have miscalculated, and it does become public, we know how to deal with it, also. Other facts will come open for review in court. All I will say, is that Mrs. Sloan will rue the day she chose this course of action against her daughter', John said.

'Mr. Stevens, I appreciate the confidence you guys have shown in me, and I will most certainly honor your request for confidentiality', the Captain answered.

CHAPTER 95

*T*hey got ready to leave the plane. 'Captain, would you take pictures of all this and send them to us. We don't have a camera and have no visual record of anything', he said.

'Sure thing! I'll give you the disk when I finish', he said.

John felt certain they would be back here before they left the area. When the FAA came in to investigate the crash, Suzie and himself would be called upon in a big way. The feds should have first priority over everything else, especially since we were there, he thought.

John tried to figure out if that priority would hinder what Suzie's mother asked to be done to her daughter immediately. A rape examination cannot wait, and since there will be a legal challenge entered against such a test, how is all this going to play out, timewise, John pondered in his mind, as he gazed around this familiar and cherished place.

'We are in for a rough ride, Suzie, when we walk out this door. 'I will do everything I can to stay by your side, but keep calm and defiant if it happens', he said.

'Don't worry, John, I'll be fine', Suzie answered.

'I want to warn you that some media people are outside. We have a press conference set up back at our base of operations, but there was a clamor to have coverage here when you two appeared, so one crew was chosen to come with us, to represent everyone at this time', Captain Baker said.

'We are ready', Suzie said, and led them out the door. A camera crew was waiting by the dying bonfire, and the captain directed them there.

He stepped before the microphone. 'We will have a brief introduction to John Stevens and Suzie Wells, in a moment. I need to remind everyone that this is a crash site, where people died, and are still here, scattered among the wreckage. Do not leave this clearing. First, this is not a news conference, so there will not be questioning', he said, as he stepped aside.

CHAPTER 96

'*I* am Suzie Wells. I am standing before you at this time, because this man, a total stranger, saved my life - twice. First, by gathering me and a bunch of seat cushions to the rear of the plane, and shielding me with his body during the crash. The second time, by anticipation that the storm we had just passed through, was coming our way, and providing a secure haven to withstand it.

Without his preparations, we would have frozen, for sure, she said. That is all I have to say'.

'I am John Stevens', he said as he stepped before the camera. 'Let me tell you a little bit about this young lady. She was alone, had just been told, by a stranger, that the plane she was on would probably crash. She did not panic, or question what I asked her to do. There was no fear in her eyes. Anxiety-yes, but she was cool. She worked beside me as we prepared for the blizzard she could not see coming. She took the word of a stranger, that we were in danger. All the details will come out later, but I have to commend Miss Wells, at this time. Thank you', he finished.

'This meeting, if I might describe it as such, is over. We are heading for the copters, and will hold the official conference as scheduled', the Captain said.

CHAPTER 97

'Suzie and I want to visit with the people in the back helicopter. We'll be with you shortly', John stated.

Mr. Brady and his crew were waiting for them. 'Were you able to pick up what was said', John asked him.

'Yes, we pushed a boom mike toward you guys, and got it all', he said.

'Captain Baker was not happy to see you, but figured it was inevitable other media would come in. Stay out of the zone, and you seem to be clear. Now, what do you want from us?', he asked.

'Everything is fine. We released our interview as soon as the other began. We'll hang around and should get clearance to cover the whole scene shortly. My boss is on their case about leaving us out of the mix', he said.

"Okay, we have to go. Just one thing. I know you are recording this. Get some good shots of our 'home', and give us a copy, please. We had no camera, so we would like anything we can get of the place', John said.

They re-joined the captain, and boarded the helicopter. 'I am really in need of a phone, John said. Any chance I can make a couple calls, I sure would be grateful', John said.

'I'll get you connected as soon as we land. The general will want to meet you first thing, but I don't know what else is planned before the media gets their shot at you. I would not be surprised to hear Social Services try to take custody of you, Ms. Wells, right away. General Simpson radioed they had contacted his headquarters several hours ago. His answer was that his command, and the FAA would require both you people for de-brief sessions, which could take days. Their reply was they would get a court order for immediate action on their demands', he said.

CHAPTER 98

'Captain Baker, can you believe this. Suzie and I have just been rescued from an ordeal as dangerous and stressful as can be endured, and we are greeted with this kind of response. I know that most of this has been generated by Suzie's mother, but court action threatened already, is bizarre. We will fight any effort to separate us. The young lady needs her attorney by her side.

We are forcing those people to go all out in their quest to vilify us. And Captain, the ploy of Mrs. Sloan is what this is all about. Suzie must be discredited as an innocent teenager. If it can be proven she engaged in sexual activities during our ordeal, then it would make it more difficult for her to claim she was always the chaste, mistreated angel, her mother says she tried to portray herself as. We shall learn the true reason a 16 year -old girl was on this airplane, alone. Believe me, Captain Baker, an awful lot is at stake here. More than finding the truth about our behavior; much more! We cannot delve any further into that matter now. It will all come out in court, Sir', he said.

'We must encourage those people to go after us, now that they have initiated the actions against us. We have nothing to fear, but you are the only one besides Suzie and I that know the facts.

There will be a lot of people who will certainly believe I molested Ms. Wells, and would continue in that belief, except for the undeniable proof that Suzie is a virgin and I could not have raped her. That will not convince all the folks that 'something' happened between us. We do not care about that. There are lots of the public who do not believe in Christian virtue, as practiced by Suzie and I. Accusations of 'brainwash' will be made against me, even child-abuse', he said.

'Right now, the more strident they become, the better for us. We don't want Mrs. Sloan to fall back on a lame excuse, that she was only trying to protect her young daughter. Those folks are convinced I am guilty, but when the truth comes out, they must be held accountable for the charges that have been leveled against both of us. They are attempting to accuse me to get at Suzie. We want them to believe they have us right now. We must make her mother look as bad as she really is', he said. 'Please trust me when I say there are very serious matters that will come out', he added.

CHAPTER 99

*P*rofessor Hamilton listened to the Sloan's press conference. The charges she brought forward were subtle. Her motives were portrayed as motherly concern for her daughter. Mr. Hamilton's reasoning was if she really wanted to protect her loved one, why would she even consider that anything like what she 'feared' had ever happened. Since he knew the truth behind the charges.

He was glad to hear her go the other way. He had no fear that John had compromised himself. He called John's grandmother. 'Thanks for your call, but I heard the news about John earlier, she said. I never believed John had died. God would not allow another such loss on me, right now. I know you might think I put such faith in my reasoning, and such a burden on the Lord, but I believe it when He said that no burden would befall his flock that would be too heavy to bear.

And I could not have borne John's loss at this time, Mr. Hamilton', she said.

'I am with you on that one, Mrs. Stevens. I never gave up believing I would see that young man again. There is another reason I called you. The young lady with John is from here. I don't know if they knew each other, or not', he said.

'I heard the girl's mother on TV, and what she said about John. I don't think for one moment John would abuse a minor girl. I have never heard John mention her, so I don't believe they knew one another'. she said.

'Mrs. Stevens, I have received some information a couple days ago in regards to Suzie Wells, and I started an investigation about her family, and I am waiting from a call from John, to find out about the charges placed against him. I will keep you informed, and I'm sure he will call you as soon as he can. Goodbye', he said.

CHAPTER 100

Mrs. Sloan had finished talking to the media. She was pleased at the way they talked about her concerns, as she described her charges. Her lawyer sitting through this event was Mr. Simmons, who had been the family attorney for some time. He was on record as opposing her stance on this issue.

'You are really taken a gamble. First, any attorney knows about the legal perils of any adult male and minor female sexual contact. John Stevens is a smart man, and would have thought of the consequences. Second, Suzie does not have to accede to your demands for examinations. If I were her lawyer, I would refuse, just because subjecting a young girl like this would be an invasion of her rights.

Third, don't you know she told him about why she was on that plane. If they fell in love, and she told him of the assault on her, he would plan their revenge on you two', he said.

'I feel certain I am right about my fear of what happened to my daughter', the mother said. 'Suzie is an exceptionally beautiful young woman. I also feel the same way about her sexual desires.

She went out of her way to seduce her stepfather. What man could resist such a woman, especially in a secluded, and closed environment they were in. That would make them both guilty, and I want to expose them to the world', she said.

CHAPTER 101

*J*ohn and Suzie boarded the helicopter, looked back one last time, and entered a new phase in their lives. They had re-entered civilization, and all the restrictions that were there, and a temporary hold on their show of emotions for each other. Maybe holding hands, but nothing more. They were going to miss the closeness they had before. Well, John sighed, it will all be waiting for them to resume, some day.

Suzie felt she knew what her 'man' was thinking as she squeezed his hand, twice. The response was so reassuring to her, yet so very sad. Two squeezes was their signal of 'I love you', and that is what she got. It was sad because hearing the words were so much better. His smile, though, made it all, just fine.

The helicopter landed inside a closed area, and they were led to a large tent, that was one of several grouped together. 'I'm General Simpson, and it is nice meeting you two', shaking hands with John and Suzie, as he led them to a seating room. 'I must say your appearance surprised all of us. We were not expecting to see such well preserved and healthy survivors of a plane crash, and a blizzard', he said.

'We were very lucky, or the Lord was watching over us, or both', John said.

The officer was struck by the appearance of Suzie, as she removed her heavy coat. He would have guessed her age much higher, except for her soft eyes, which were stunningly greenish. They showed anxiety, but were alert. Everyone in the room was well aware of her, but it was quite clear that those eyes were focused on John. That and her body language, an ever so slight leaning toward the man.

General Simpson had hoped these young folks could overcome the charges hurled at them by the girl's mother, but it was obvious they cared about each other in a more than a casual manner.

CHAPTER 102

'*I* need to make several important calls, General Simpson', John said.

'Sure thing. The phone is on that table. We'll leave you alone, but try to make it short. The media is waiting', he said.

They left the area, as John dialed his grandmother. 'I have been following everything on the TV, John. Professor Hamilton has been in touch. You know, we both never doubted you had survived, and were alive', she said.

'Suzie and I have fallen in love, Grandma. She has been terribly abused by her family, and we are going to ask the courts to terminate their parental connection. We are hoping you would agree to offer to become her guardian. We plan on a wedding after she becomes an adult; i.e., age wise.

She already is a mature young lady, and I love her', he said.

'Of course, I will, John, and be proud to do so', she answered. 'I have to go now. Bye', he said.

CHAPTER 103

*P*rofessor Hamilton answered the phone on the first ring. He was waiting for this call. 'Hello, Sir, this is my first chance to call you. We just got to a staging area, so I don't know what they will do with us', John said.

'Let me bring you up to date on matters at home, John. You know I am pleased to hear your voice. I held to the hope you had survived. I look forward to hearing the story of that adventure. Now, about Suzie. I imagine she told you the full tale concerning her family. Bill Owens is the neighbor Suzie ran to after escaping her stepfather's assault. He called me before they found you guys, after seeing me on television talking about passengers on your ill-fated flight; namely, you and Suzie. He had also listened to Mrs. Sloan's comments about her missing daughter, which did not match with what happened at his house. His narrative set me on an investigation into the incident. I got depositions from him, and his neighbor, who also witnessed Suzie's encounter with her family at Mr. Owens' house', he said.

'That is great, Sir. We are going to bury those two for what they have done, and are doing, to Suzie. Right now, I need an attorney in this area, and one there. I think you know Joe Greene. He was Dad's lawyer. Get him on board, if you can. I won't be able to freely use the phone for a - while, so I need your help. I want to start court proceedings to vacate the Sloan's parental control over Suzie. Also, start an inquiry in regards to Suzie's father's will. She informed me that she did not receive anything from her father's estate. Inform everyone that Suzie and I will fight, in court, any attempt to deny the young lady, her civil rights. Gotta go, Sir. Thanks for everything', he said.

CHAPTER 104

*T*he general led them toward another, larger tent. 'The media is assembled in here. I'll start it off and turn it over to you guys', he said.

Before they could leave the first tent, Captain Baker approached the two. 'There is a gentleman here who says he is your attorney', he said.

'Yes, that would be Sam Browne', John said.

Professor Hamilton had told John he would be contacting the man. He gave John a brief history; he finished his main career in the southern states, and had semi-retired up here. He was a robust looking, heavy-set older man. The easy way he carried himself suggested an athletic background, and his eyes radiated confidence. They shook hands all around, and John got down to business.

'Mr. Browne, I know you are aware of our problems, and why we need your services. Tell us what you have heard', John said.

'You two are the talk of the town, so to speak. It is non-stop on every television station, and radio and he press are on the story full time. I have covered the whole thing, especially since talking to Professor Hamilton. He filled me in on both your backgrounds, and I watched your mother, Suzie. What a performance she put on', he said.

'Well, you will begin in a few minutes, addressing the media for us. Suzie and I will not answer any questions about our personal interplay during our ordeal. We will talk about the crash to the authorities fully, as long as it is about the flight, and our survival. We are headed to court, and you will represent us both. No media appearances for us until all legal matters are settled. We will fill you in as soon as you get through your meeting with the media', John said.

'Make sure they understand there will be no discussion at all, period. Now, in regards to our reactions to medical procedures being performed on Ms. Wells. We will fight this all the way. We will object to every action concerning this issue, with no discussion on our part. We want an all-out effort on their behalf pertaining to this subject. The real reason for this offensive campaign is to degrade Ms. Well's character; to portray her as a sexual degenerate. The more they push this theme, the harder they fall. When the truth is known, we don't intend to allow them to be able to fall back on the lame excuse that they were only concerned about Ms. Well's reputation, and her welfare', he said.

CHAPTER 105

*N*ow, here is our planned course of action, Mr. Browne. Suzie intends to have two examinations to clear her of any charges, or suggestions about her virginity. One by the eventual order of the courts, and one by a prominent expert doctor at home', he said.

Suzie spoke up. 'I want you, Mr. Browne, to feel comfortable, and secure in defending John and me, regarding our conduct toward each other. I am a virgin, as I was taught by my father, and my Christian faith, to remain chaste. John's teaching were exactly as mine, so it was easy to honor both our fathers', she said.

Mr. Browne sat across from these kids, and wondered how he could be so lucky and thrilled to be a part of what was about to be unfurled to the world. As an attorney, he had dreamed of being on such a drama. Now, he was ready to represent his clients.

CHAPTER 106

M r. Browne entered the room, and was met by an army captain. 'I'm Captain Baker. 'Where are Mr. Stevens and Ms. Wells?', he asked.

'They will not be coming. I am their attorney and will represent them', he said.

'Mr. Stevens and Ms. Wells will not be available for any public appearances at this time. Due to the accusations thrown at them, all public statements to the media have been put on hold. They will meet with authorities concerning the accident.

My clients have been cooperative with everyone from the moment they were found. They were thrown together through no action of theirs. Yet, this accidental association is being turned into a sinister affair. How grossly unfair can you get', he said. He turned and left the room.

Captain baker was stunned by the attorney's announcement concerning John's decision about the media. Yet, he could understand their strategy. They must have an overwhelming victory regarding Mrs. Sloan's accusations. Without solid proof of their innocence, the lives of them both would forever be tainted. Even if they were exonerated, many people would still doubt their story.

The captain wondered why a mother would tarnish the life of her child in this way. John had mentioned that there were other matters involved in this affair. Well, time will tell, he thought. Right now, he had to face an upset media.

'Folks, we have to respect John and Suzie in their delay in speaking to you. We should be able to understand how devastating Suzie must feel. Right now, the two young, people are meeting with federal investigators, as the search begins for cause, or causes, of the crash of flight 078. I cannot give you a time-table of events at this moment. Questions now', he said.

'When they finish with questions about the crash, where will they go?', a reporter asked.

'I am not sure, the captain answered. The social services agency has demanded Suzie be turned over to them, immediately. They already have a court order, but their attorney, Mr. Browne, indicated there would be an appeal to any such action. Next', he said.

'We would like a photo session with Mr. Stevens and Ms. Wells. Will you bring them out?', another asked.

'I will urge the two to avail themselves for such an occasion. I am to be notified the minute they finish with the investigators', he said. "Look, I know you have a lot of questions, but let me go check, and make sure I can corral them for you. Sit tight for a while', he said.

CHAPTER 107

*C*aptain baker met John and Suzie as they left the room. The questions had all been answered. 'Captain, I need some time with our attorney right now, afterwards, we will meet the press', he said.

'Mr. Browne, we are going to fill you in on everything right now. First, Suzie will shortly be making a serious accusation of sexual assault on her by her stepfather. This attack happened the day before she was put on the plane by her mother, exiled from her home, destined to never return. She had a one-way ticket to her father's family. Professor Hamilton has depositions from two men who saw Ms. Wells immediately after the assault. Suzie escaped the man before any damages occurred, except torn clothes. She ran to a neighbor's house, asking for help.

Professor Hamilton will fill you in on all the details later. Her parents did not report this molestation to anyone', he said.

'This is the main reason for Mrs. Sloan's actions now. She desperately needs to brand Suzie a delinquent, as a defense for her husband's actions. We are going to destroy those people, by their own deeds, Mr. Browne', he said.

'Secondly, the professor is asking the courts at home, to vacate Mrs. Sloan's parental rights. We need to separate them for good', John said.

'Third, Ms. Wells was excluded from her father's estate. He died a couple years ago, but Suzie never received a penny. The professor is on this matter, also. You can go before the media right now, to fill them in on our plans up here, but we want to wait on our charges, until we see what happens here. You can advise them Suzie and I will be filing civil suits against the Sloans. I am Ms. Wells personal attorney, and will fight all efforts to separate us. I shall demand to be present at her side at all times. If you have any contacts in this area, please call on them. We will need the help', he said. 'One question surely will be asked. Were Suzie and I acquainted in any way before the plane encounter. The answer is - no. We had not even heard of each other. I was a little upset that my athletic prowess had escaped her notice, but I put it down as being caused by her young age', he said.

CHAPTER 108

Suzie and John entered the press room for the photo session. John knew there would be questions, and was undecided about how to handle them. 'We'll see how it goes, Suzie. You may want to answer some of them, as long as they are not personal, but feel free to do anything you desire. Just don't think you need my approval, lovely lady. But be careful, because they will try their best to get us to talk', he said.

'I am John Stevens and this young lady is Suzie Wells. We are here for you to see the couple who survived the plane crash. We do not want to answer any personal questions, or any about our ordeal. We will leave if you disregard our request', he said. 'We have valid reasons for asking this, so there is no need for any of you to be upset about it. In due time, we will tell our story', he said.

CHAPTER 109

*H*ere was the story of the year, maybe ten years. It could be the story of the century. And those people say - no questions? Everyone in the press room shook their collective heads, in disbelief. 'That mother made headlines, but she sure made a mess of this situation. We know she is the reason that couple clammed up. Now, we must sit around, trying to dig for any little tidbit to write about. I'll end up submitting a story of that crew going to the crash site, and getting an interview, and I won't be the only one. The cheats are being treated like celebrities. Everyone thinks they got a big story with the promise to sit on it awhile', the reporter said.

CHAPTER 110

M r. Browne had been very busy, since John had given him all the facts of the case. His first call was to the governor's office. The man was a good friend and a political compadre.

'I want to speak to the boss', he told the secretary. After a very short wait, the governor was on the phone. 'I have been expecting your call. When I saw where you got employed on the most important case you or I will ever see', he said.

'Then, you know why I am calling, sir. This couple is going to create a much bigger storm than the one just finished. What you know isn't the whole story. There is more to come, and it is all bad news for Mrs. Sloan. Mr. Stevens is saving his bomb-shell for later. I am to resist in court the effort of the state to take her into custody. We will fight any order to breach her civil rights. Your Honor, our actions are a smoke-screen. I tell you this in confidentiality, and on this phone I know to be secure. You are probably going to be asked to intervene at some time, so I want to assure you that Mr. Stevens and Ms. Wells will be exonerated. You can choose your action, knowing that fact. Social services is ready to pounce on Ms. Wells. We will appeal, but we don't care what they do, because the outcome is not in doubt', he said.

'Okay, I'll watch and act when it is appropriate', the governor replied.

CHAPTER 111

*E*very news outlet either took pictures, or asked questions. Suzie and John kept a smile on their faces, posed separately, and together, and refused to acknowledge the questioners. They were followed to the podium by their lawyer, Sam Browne.

'I heard a lot of questions asked of Mr. Stevens and Ms. Wells. You were told they would not respond, so no need to get upset. The social services people have demanded Ms. Wells be turned over to them, and have a court order to that effect. We object strenuously that the order was issued without our participation in the procedure, and we have appealed. Ms. Well's attorney, in her home town, has petitioned the courts there, to have the young lady's parental ties be terminated from her mother. The lawyer, Mr. Joe Greene, has also filed, at Suzie's request, a petition to name Mrs. Stevens, her guardian. Mrs. Stevens is the grandmother of John Stevens.

We contend that Mrs. Sloan has forfeited all rights by her accusations, and the blatantly cruel act of putting her daughter, alone, on this ill-fated flight, will be shown to be a punitive move against the teen-ager.

Charges of a very serious nature related to these issues, are pending. That is all I have, at this time', he said.

CHAPTER 112

*J*oe Greene had just watched the latest news. The two local young folks were the talk of the town. Now, this new development from Suzie Well's mother added more interest to the story. He knew of John Stevens from his football days at the university, and as a protege of Dr. Hamilton. 'You have a call from Professor Hamilton', the secretary announced. 'Dr. Hamilton, I was this very moment thinking about you. Your former student is all over the media', he said. 'I suppose John has contacted you'.

'Yes, he has, and they are both fine, but they need a lot of help. John has retained counsel, where they are now. And he needs an attorney here. Are you available to represent both of them?', he asked.

'Wow, what a break', Joe hollered. 'Thank you, Professor, I sure am'.

'Okay, here's the deal. There are three issues. First, to petition the court to have John's grandmother, Anne Stevens, named as Suzie's guardian. This request is because of the other two items. Ms. Wells will shortly accuse her stepfather of attempted rape. This happened a couple days before her mother put her on that plane. The third, is the estate of Suzie's late father. The only child of that man never received anything. Come by my office for all the details. Put your investigative team on this immediately', he said.

CHAPTER 113

John and Suzie had just finished their meeting with the folks investigating the crash. Everything went along fine. Since there were survivors who could tell them what happened, it took far less time to get to the cause, or causes. Along with the black box data, the weather, and the site, John and Suzie filled in the missing pieces. Their conclusions were that the plane was struck by lightning, knocking out all the communications, and most of the controls.

'It's amazing how you folks were able to pick the one spot where you could survive. An awful lot of luck was on your side', he said. The two young people didn't say anything, but hand squeezes between them, and their silent prayers were thanks to the Lord. He was their 'luck'.

Their attorney, Sam Browne, was waiting for them. He filled them in on the actions of the state's child welfare agency. 'They got a Judge to rubber-stamp the demand for Ms. Wells to be turned over to them. I have another Judge, and he is ready to over -ride the order. I was about to call him', he said.

'Did the order mention my desire to have my attorney, Mr. Stevens, with me at all times?', Suzie asked.

'No, there is no such granting of that request', Mr. Browne answered. 'Okay, we will not object to the order, as long as I am allowed to be with Suzie. We want this action to proceed, but with the notion that we are afraid. You know how to play that game, Sam. Dr. Hamilton told me all about you, He said that you are the best he ever heard before a jury. We'll wait here for your return', John said.

CHAPTER 114

M s. Stone, the director of the state child services agency, saw Mr. Browne walk toward them. She was well acquainted with the lawyer and his reputation. She knew he was a big buddy of the governor and was a powerful political figure. She did not look forward to this meeting, since she knew who he was representing.

'I am Mr. Sam Browne, the attorney for Ms. Suzie Wells', he said. 'I have no desire for any further introductions, so let's get down to business. I am aware of your order from that lackey Judge   of yours, and if this were not such a serious matter, I would make you eat his 'edict', without   salt. But, right now, we will allow this order from the court, if Ms. Wells' request to have her attorney accompany her at all time is granted', he stated. With his hands on his hips, his feet wide apart, and his huge body fully erect, Mr. Browne was an imposing figure. 'Deny our one request, and you have a fight on your hands. I don't want any dilly-dally, just a straight answer- Right now', he demanded.

Ms. Stone could not think, under these conditions. She knew if the man did not get an answer, and very soon, this whole matter would come apart. Ms. Wells had to be examined very soon, or the procedure would be useless. The condition they wanted imposed was not unusual or extreme, but to have a lawyer looking over their shoulder would restrict them immensely. 'Okay, your request is granted.

When can Ms. Wells and you be available?', she asked.

'I am not Ms. Wells' personal attorney. Mr. John Stevens is, and they are ready now', he said.

She had just been given the shock of her life. The man they were trying to hang for statutory rape was to be in the room with them all the time, as they tried to find the evidence to conflict him, by going after the young lady about to be examined.

'This is about to become a very stressful endeavor', she told her staff. 'Keep everything low-key and be calm. Mr. Stevens could be waiting for a mistake on our part, to cause trouble for us. We must not show any emotion, one way or the other', she said.

Ms. Stone shuddered at the thought, of how her own teen-aged daughter would react to this type of invasion on her body. She did not relish this moment, but it was her job to do, she thought.

CHAPTER 115

*T*he young couple came through the door. Ms. Stone and her staff were not prepared for what they saw. Ms. Wells was strikingly beautiful, a much more mature looking young lady than they had expected. Mr. Stevens was as handsome as Suzie was pretty.

Both walked with a regal air of confidence, demanding attention and respect. None of them had ever been a part of an event like this. All of the staff were female, several near the age of the man in front of them, and they were struck by his appearance.

Ms. Stone spoke up quickly, introducing herself. 'Let's get on with this. The two of you and myself will ride together to the hospital for the examination. Everything is ready and waiting for us, Ms. Wells', she said.

CHAPTER 116

Mr. Browne stepped before the assembled media. 'The prisoner and her attorney are headed to the hospital with her jailer, so she can be stripped of all her clothes, and her dignity. All at the behest of a depraved parent. Now, some of you learned Journalist majors are going to report that the following facts I am about to give you, are acts of revenge against that person, by my clients. Well, they are not.

These actions were delayed, so as not to discourage this upcoming examination. Yes, you heard me correctly. I said my clients want this action to proceed' he said.

'Now, for my news. Ms. Wells has directed her attorney, Mr. Joe Greene, to contact authorities in her home town and advise them that she is charging Mr. Bill Sloane, her stepfather, with attempted rape. This event happened prior to her plane ride. Evidence will be presented that this attack was the reason her mother put her on that flight. This alleged molestation charge is also the reason this procedure is being performed on Ms. Wells. This 'mother' is trying to paint a picture of her teenaged daughter as a sexual pervert, by first enticing her innocent husband, and secondly, having an affair with Mr. Stevens', he said.

'Ms. Wells is also petitioning the court to vacate her mother's parental rights. Last, Ms. Wells is asking for a review of her late father's will. The only child of a devoted and loving father should have received at least a penny from his estate', he said.

The attorney was being bombarded with dozens of questions at one time. Those reporters were clamoring for answers, while others were on the phone to their editors, while all the cameras were on the lawyer. 'Folks, let me answer your inquiries this way. The two people involved in this matter will be available as soon as possible, so hold everything until they get here', Sam concluded.

CHAPTER 117

*T*hose two people had arrived at the hospital, and were greeted by dozens of media, each demanding answers. They had been given Ms. Wells' attorneys statements and were seeking an interview from the couple. However, Ms. Stone hustled them into a waiting room, and were met by several members of the hospital staff, that included Dr. Shamblee, head physician. The doctor introduced himself, and began explaining to Suzie the procedure they would follow with her.

At that time, John interrupted. 'Please excuse for just a moment. I want to speak to Ms. Wells', he said. John led her to the far corner of the room, holding her hand as they walked. 'I will be leaving you now, Suzie. You are in a nice place, and they are going to look after you. I'll be right here when you finish', he said. He squeezed her hand two times, and got the same in return, plus a beautiful smile.

'We have just now been alone for quite a-while and I have missed your hand signals', Suzie said, plus I am nervous about this, John. I know it will turn out okay, I've never been examined before', she said. 'I know, darling. If there were another way to handle this, I would not allow this to happen', John said.

Everyone was standing around, waiting, and watching, so the sudden urge to grab this man in a bear-hug, had to be stifled. 'You called me 'darling'. It is really hard to keep reminding myself that I have only known you for about one week, when you use those sweet, meaningful words of endearment. I'm not used to them, but they have the most profound effect on me, and I just want to shower you with hugs and kisses', she whispered.

They stood there holding hands in a casual manner, as seen by their audience, but they both were squeezing as fast as they could, telling each other of their love.

'I'll be waiting for you, he said.

CHAPTER 118

*D*r. Shamblee resumed his discussion with Suzie about how the examination would be conducted. 'We will be as brief as possible, Ms. Wells. Young ladies your age rarely have this type procedure, except in cases of rape'.

'Doctor, I was not raped, so why are you doing this', Suzie asked.

'This hospital does not condone this action. We are forced to comply with the court order, and you did agree to having it done', he said.

'All this is against my will, but I want to clear my name, and by doing so, I clear Mr. Stevens. Everything else means nothing to me. That wonderful man did not save us, just to be condemned for something he never did. Let's get this over with, Dr. Shamblee', she said.

CHAPTER 119

Ms. Stone was joined at this time by a man she recognized as the local district attorney, Mr. Jack Stanford. 'I am here to take Mr. Stevens to jail as soon as they finish with Ms. Wells', he said.

'Isn't that a bit presumptuous on your part?', she said.

'No, I am convinced he is guilty, and if he is, you will have to take charge of the girl. We are going to be big news; even more than right now. I have my speech already', he said.

The same sense of confidence was being expressed by Mrs. Sloan. 'I know it looks bad for us now, but everything will change when Suzie comes out of the hospital. It'll be her word against yours. She will remain my minor child, and we will be able to defend our decision on the handling of her father's estate. We should be famous enough to capitalize on all this publicity by writing a book', she said.

She, her husband and their lawyer were seated in front of the television, watching them head to the examination room. They saw John take her aside, and it was evident to them all, that the two were lovers. The body language, the looks they exchanged, and the way they held hands, was a dead give-away of their feelings and intimacy.

'You better pray all you say is true, because if not, you two are history. I know you will keep on fighting, even though John is cleared of molesting Suzie, but what they went through together, along with this attack on their behavior during this miraculous survival, will have the whole world cheering for them. You cannot win attacking them any further', the lawyer sermonized.

'I cannot foresee any jury convicting Mr. Stevens of anything he could have done during their trapped confinement, unless Ms. Wells is the accuser. Doesn't seem very likely that will happen', he said.

CHAPTER 120

*S*uzie walked into the examination room with the hospital personnel ready to complete their task. Dr. Shamblee was the only male present.

'My one request is that no males be here, if you don't mind', she said.

'That is fine, Ms. Wells, Dr. Shamblee said. Let me introduce the two female doctors, and one nurse, who will do the work. Dr. Metcalf will start the examination, Dr. Smith will take the smears needed to identify any foreign DNA in or around your pelvic area. After Dr. Metcalf finishes, she will put her conclusions in the computer without making any oral statements. Then, Dr. Smith will examine you exactly as Dr. Metcalf did', she said.

'We want a back-up opinion, as there is sure to be efforts by some people to discredit our work, regardless of the outcome. Dr. Smith will not divulge her findings. She will put everything in the computer, also. The entire hospital's staff will then review the two reports. If there is any discrepancy, we will ask your permission to allow Dr. Shamblee to examine you', she said.

'I am glad you are making this effort to be fair. I was very afraid coming here as to how I was going to be treated. I told you why I want to clear this matter, for John's sake. It is alright for Dr. Shamblee to examine me. In fact, I want him to do it, no matter what. That way, it would be extremely difficult for anyone to have further doubts about John and my self's behavior', she said. 'Let's get this over with, please?

'Okay, young lady, here we go', Dr. Metcalf said.

CHAPTER 121

*T*he media came to attention, as a large body of the hospital personnel entered the room. 'I am Dr. Steinberg, head doctor of this hospital. The examination of Ms. Wells is concluded. I really should have said-examinations, since three doctors independently were involved. Two were scheduled by the hospital. Each was performed separately by Dr. Metcalf and Dr. Smith. Their reports were entered into the computer and analyzed for any differences. Before the results were known, Ms. Wells requested that Dr. Shamblee also examine her. I will let each read the reports submitted', he said.

'I am Dr. Metcalf. My report: I find no evidence what-so-ever of any penetration of the subject', she read.

'Dr. Smith here, and my report is: Absolutely a virgin young woman. No question, period', she said.

'My role in this affair was to be the third examiner, in case of differences that may have been found in the originals. Before any results were known, Ms. Wells asked me to examine her. She stated that her request was made to have overwhelming proof Mr. Stevens, or any other male, had ever touched her. My examination showed that to be true, as for as the purity of this young lady', he said.

'This hospital was forced to invade and violate this teenager's body. We did what was demanded of us. 'I just want to say to anyone who doubts this young lady, is either an utter fool, or is mentally deranged. Thank you, and goodbye', he ended.

To the surprise of everyone, the whole body of reporters, cameramen, announcers, and crew members, were silent until the director of the hospital finished. Then, the whole place erupted in cheers, and applause.

The only person who remained motionless, was Jack Stanford, the district attorney. He had been assured by Suzie's mother, that the verdict of the exam would be the opposite of what he had just heard. She had painted her daughter as a perverted delinquent, devoid of decent morals.

Something was not right, he reasoned. He was a fair and competent administrator of his office, but he had let the possibility of national recognition cloud his normal conservatism and resist the rush to judgement.

He approached Sam Browne, who was standing alone on the other side of the room. 'Well, as you know, Sam, I was ready to do my job, in case things had been different', he said.

'Yeah, all primed to bask in the bright glow of sensationalism, you mean. Mrs. Sloan surely called you with convincing arguments against her daughter, and you bite. Not like that staid DA I know', Sam said.

'You are exactly right, sir. I should have been wary of a mother having such hatred toward her offspring. There is something else in play, and you could help a dumb yoyo, if you would', Jack said.

'Later, maybe. Right now, I have to meet with my clients. I think they have had enough time alone. I can't imagine the pressure, both mental, and physical, they have been under. They are obviously in love, so I'd better show up, and quickly', he said.

John was standing in the same spot where he and Suzie had last parted. He knew what the outcome of the exam would be. His trust in her was total belief. She saw him as she came out the door, and ran unashamed into his arms. As their bodies came together, a sense of shock overcame them. For the second time in the short time they had known each other, they had come in contact with one another without layers and layers of clothing between them.

The first time would forever be etched in their memories, as John put himself over her to protect her from the crash. That act had stolen her heart, and her reaction was one of love. This encounter shook them both to the core of their being, for the reaction was sexual. Neither had ever experienced such a surge of emotion, and it jolted them apart.

They stood still, holding each other's arms, and looking at one another in awe. Slowly, a smile came to Suzie's face. 'We have just cleared one hurdle, and I thought it was a tough one, but our next one will be quite demanding, won't it', she whispered in his ear.

'Yes, it will, my beautiful darling', he answered.

CHAPTER 122

*T*his whole scene was being broadcast around the world, unbeknown to the two lovers. A dozen or more network type cameras were focused on them, along with dozens of others. They became aware of the outside horde when the mass completely surrounded them, and the flashes blinded their eyes.

'We did compose ourselves somewhat', Suzie said.

'These people are expecting a word or two from you guys', Sam said. He had arrived with the media, and had witnessed the interaction between the couple. It could have been caused by the relief of the good results of Suzie's exam, but no one in that room believed that scenario. It was obvious to the world, those two were in love.

'Suzie and I want to say that we hope this ordeal imposed on her will satisfy the authorities pertaining to our conduct during our confinement together. The morals and faith of Ms. Wells would have never allowed any actions on her part, or mine, that would have been detrimental to herself. Several very dramatical events occurred while we were together. We were teetering on the edge of an abyss, as close to death as anyone could ever be. The trust she showed in me began just before the crash, and continued unabated throughout the time we were isolated from civilization. I love this woman with all my heart', he said.

'I want every one of the women in this room to take a good look at John Stevens. Put yourself in my shoes. You don't have to consider what he did, just tell me- could you love this man? I didn't stand a chance. It was, literally, love at first sight on my part, and this is the truth; I feel I am the luckiest woman in the world', she said.

John spoke up. 'I have asked her to marry me, and she has accepted my proposal. It will be several years before our wedding, as we wait for her to grow up. Look at her now. I can't imagine what she will 'grow up' to be. Oh, well, that's the chance I have to take. You have to take what you get', he laughed

'Seriously, we have told you of our devotion to each other, and our future plans, somewhat. We still a few problems awaiting us. We will not be answering any questions regarding our stay in the plane wreckage. Our lives together will remain private, both now and later on. We will let Mr. Browne, our attorney, say a few words', John said.

'It is nice to have this phase of the investigation concerning Mr. Stevens and Ms. Wells over and done with. Yes, I said 'phase'. There is a lot more to come, and here is the first part: Mrs. Sloan, the mother of Ms. Wells, was trying to blow a smoke screen, when she demanded the test be conducted on her daughter. I am sure some of you, at least, questioned why Suzie was on that ill-fated airplane, alone, in the middle of the winter', he said.

'Well, here is the reason. Bill Sloan, Suzie's stepfather, had just attempted to rape the young lady. Mr. Joe Greene, Suzie's attorney in her home town, will be presenting all the details to the authorities there shortly. He will ask for charges to be brought against the man, as the perpetrator, and the woman, as an accessory, after the fact. She wanted Ms. Wells portrayed as a perverted, amoral teenager. Mr. Sloan is trying to defend himself as the prey of a demented child.

Other actions will also be initiated. Now, these young people have just been through a whole lot, and we are going to retire from the scene, until tomorrow', he said.

CHAPTER 123

Captain Baker greeted Suzie and John as they left the media room. 'You told me how this day would end, did you not. We were all pulling for you. Well, most everyone. There will always be those on the other side of the fence, so to speak. I have this disc for you, with pictures of the crash scene', he said.

'The airline is attempting to buy about twenty acres that will include the whole area around the tail section, which they intend to preserve and make into a park. All the land for miles in each direction is federally owned, so you may be looking at a future national park. If that happens, you are sure to be asked to dedicate it. The inside will remain as you left it. I can imagine years from now revisiting the place', he said. 'I will always remember hearing the pilot who found you guys telling us there were two survivors. My thought was- how could that be possible. And here you are. It is the story of the century. All kind of tales will be invented over the years, so it is great news you have everything written down', he said. 'There will be people and stories coming out of the woodwork, trying to cash in, or get their 15 minutes of fame'.

'Oh, John, isn't that great news', Suzie said. 'Yes, it certainly is, and for another reason also. I have all my notes recording our hours here, and I intend to write a book, detailing the whole story. When they agree to make a movie later, they will have their set ready-made', he said. Maybe you will be given the part to play yourself. The role wouldn't require any acting skill on your part. Hey, I like that', he said.

'You are crazy. No way that could happen. Besides, I have other plans for my life. After two years of school, I hope to get married and start a family. How does that grab you, mister?', she said.

'Well, I say you don't have to hope about the marriage bit, And I hope you start out having a girl, because she would have to be the beauty queen of the maternity ward', he said.

CHAPTER 124

*P*rofessor Hamilton and Joe Greene were on the phone. They had just finished a conference call with John. 'I know you saw the news session we had. Suzie and I did not intend to air our emotion that way. It is pretty wild up here, in regards to the media, but we are fine. How are things going down your way?', he asked.

'John, this city is jumping. You guys are the talk of the town. The headline on the front page was: 'They passed the test'. Quite a show. Too bad that shoved your rescue and return story all the way off the front page. Give the folks a hint of a sex scandal, and they go berserk. You sure took the winds out of that mother's sails', the lawyer answered. 'We have everything moving forward. The results up your way paves the path for action soon. Maybe tomorrow on the parental motion, and I'm sure that is number one on the list', he said.

'Yes, it is. The social services up here want to take Suzie, I'm certain. No action yet, but the local DA had me in handcuffs, at least in his mind, so he is looking for anything to save face. Sam is ready to counter anything they try. He is in touch with the governor concerning that guy, whom he hates. Push as hard as you can, because you know we can't leave here until Suzie is free of her mother's control.

I'll talk to you tomorrow, Mr. Hamilton. Thanks for everything', he said.

CHAPTER 125

'*I* cannot believe the results of Suzie's exam', her mother said. 'I want to contest the whole thing. Our future rested on the outcome', she said.

'Maybe you will remember I spoke to you about what would happen if this very thing occurred', the lawyer said. 'There is a court hearing today you are well aware of. Suzie's attorney will win that case, and you will no longer have custody of your daughter. I would suggest you make every effort to placate her. Don't fight this case, and maybe they will ease up on you. I really would not count on it, though. The alleged assault charges are the killers. I don't know why I have continued as your attorney, since you failed to inform me of the witnesses to the incident. You were so sure that your daughter was a delinquent, I guess, was the reason', he said. 'On the other hand, I really find your conduct lacks any moralistic values, therefore, I will advise the court that I no longer am your attorney. So long, and goodbye', he said.

CHAPTER 126

*T*he head man of the investigation team was addressing the media. 'The fact that we had two eye-witnesses to the crash, made our job much easier. We learned, with a very high probability guess, that a lightning strike crippled the plane's electronics, and some of the controls. Mr. Stevens foresaw the danger, and herded Ms. Wells, along with as many of the seat cushions as they could carry, to the rear of the plane. There is a bulkhead separating the aft galley from the passenger area. John piled the cushions against that wall, put Suzie on them, and then placed himself on top of her. This action kept them from being thrown around, and saved their lives. Even though the tail section survived, the sudden jolt of the impact would have propelled them against the plane's wall, had they not been jammed as they were', he said.

'Mr. Stevens also was correct in his evaluation of the storm's path, surmising it was headed their way. By working to seal the open end of the plane's remnant in advance, they were able to weather the worst winter blizzard on record. It really bothered most of us on this team, which all this effort and wisdom seemed to be forgotten, in the attempt to hang this young man. We are so pleased they beat this rap. He should be awarded a medal, and I am going to recommend that action be taken, by the president', he concluded.

CHAPTER 127

'*I* am pleased to report that your grandmother is now the legal guardian of Ms. Suzie Wells', Professor Hamilton announced.

John was on the phone, having called for just that information. 'Wonderful news, and thanks so much, Professor. We will be headed home as soon as possible. It may be a couple days before everything is cleared up here. These people are sure to want written proof before releasing Suzie. Sam will call the governor for help in speeding up the process', he said. 'The sale of dad's business is still pending. I need to stop that action, because I intend to take over the management.

I cannot leave our town, since Suzie will be there, Mr. Hamilton. It is impossible for me to realize it has only been a couple weeks since the funeral. So much has happened, it makes my head spin, sir. The Lord has truly blessed Suzie and I, and we are so grateful', he said.

John and Suzie had just gotten off the phone with the professor. They were not in a mood to celebrate. It was both good and bad news. John knew how it was to lose a parent, and that is what Suzie was experiencing right now. He put his arm around her as she began to cry. She felt her loss was the end of her relationship with her mother, and the thought was heart-breaking for the young teenager.

John held her until the tears subsided.

Suzie, I know you still love your mother, and I believe she loves you. Sometimes people lose their way in life, striving for a certain goal and forgetting other things for a-while. That is what she has done, and now her life is in shambles. Let's you and I, together, see what we can do to help her find her way again. If we make the effort, and fail, we will better ourselves for the trying. But, we may not fail, and who can tell how things will turn out between us all', he said.

The thoughts that were now running around in her head, the possibility of some type of relationship with her mother, would have never occurred to her without John's help. The ray of hope shining down upon her troubled soul was just what she needed.

'I forgot that I not only have you, but I can call upon the Lord, in times of need. I feel so much better, John. Maybe she does love me, because I do love her, I just don't like her right now', she said.

'How easy does it become to forgive, when you have the Lord in your heart. I guess there is not much room left for hate or revenge when you are filled with the Holy Spirit, and the love for an angel', John said.

They both put aside all thoughts of those seemingly trivial things, and turned to each other. Words like that make my heart sing, Suzie thought. 'Yes, my sweetheart, I love you, too', she cooed.

CHAPTER 128

*T*hey both could hardly sleep last night. For the first time since the crash, they were apart, in separate beds, and in different rooms. It hit them both, when the captain showed them those sleeping quarters. They had not even thought about it. John looked at Suzie and she looked at him, and just stood there, along with the captain, who had no clue what was happening.

'Captain, you have confronted us with a situation we had completely overlooked. We have been sleeping, all bundled in clothes to keep warm, together since we met. It just dawned on us that we can no longer do that', John said.

Suzie burst out laughing. That started John on a gaggle of his own, filling the hall with their uproar. Several doors opened, as Captain Baker joined the couple's guffaws. 'Please don't tell on us, sir. We are truly two dumb kids. Worn out, mentally drained, and ready to go home.

Otherwise, we're okay', John said.

'Well, it was fortunate I was here, or some of those people we aroused, might have called the MP's, and you could have been charged with disturbing the peace. Go to your rooms, and mind your manners', he said, laughing.

They went to Suzie's room to say their goodnights. 'This is going to be a long, lonely night, John. We thought we were marooned before, trapped in our little shelter from the tempest, but it turned out to be our paradise, our sanctuary', she said. John held her for a moment, lightly kissed her goodnight, and left.

CHAPTER 129

*C*aptain Baker was eating when John and Suzie entered the dining room. He was alone, so they sat at his table.

'I am to take you folks to town today, so you can catch a plane home. We booked you on the same airline, mainly because it's the only one flying this way', the captain said.

'That's great. We are ready to go. We have a couple lives to renew, although I don't see how we are going to recognize them. It feels as if I just started living. You have been our salvation, Captain. I hate saying goodbye. Please give us your address, and we will keep in touch, if you want. I notice all the media people with their cameras focused on you', he said.

The press coverage you have received should get you a promotion', Suzie said.

'That's not the way it works, Suzie. General Simpson is the big hero. As they say- Rank has it's privileges. For me, it's another mission. But, this one has turned out to be special, I must say. Those reporters want to know everything we ever talked about. You can't believe the questions they ask. I refer them to the general, because he loves the limelight. Good thing you didn't confide in him. Maybe we'll meet again. I like you two kids', he said.

CHAPTER 130

*J*ohn held Suzie's hand as they walked toward flight 079. The same type plane, and the return trip of flight 078, the ill-fated one that brought them together. Strangers, with little purpose in either of their lives. Now, the airport was packed with people, mainly to see them on their way. A pair now; not strangers, and with big plans.

The plane ride was flawless, and the weather was great. All during the trip, other passengers asked them for their autographs and wanted to chat about their experiences.

'I suppose this is something we are to expect for some time', John said.

'We will learn how to handle the attention with this type of display. We have become celebrities in our own right', Suzie said.

One of the pilots approached the couple and sat down next to Suzie. 'I don't want to remind you of your ordeal, but my best friend was the captain on your flight. I read the report you submitted describing the last moments of the plane's descent. You praised the pilot's actions. Thank you for those words for my friend. When his family found out you would be on this plane, his wife gave me this letter to give you', he said.

'I'm not going to open this right now, Captain, if you don't mind. This is too public a place. I see where she has put her address on the note, so I'll send her a reply', John said.

'That's fine. It would mean a whole lot to her', the pilot replied.

CHAPTER 131

'The first thing I must do after we get settled in, my dear, is to get your engagement ring. Dad had a suite at his office, complete with everything. I will stay there. I don't want to live with you and grandma. Mom and dad both had a car, and they are parked at the house. I couldn't find in my heart to sell them before I left, so we will have transportation', John said.

CHAPTER 132

*A*mong the large crowd that were there to meet them after deplaning, were Professor Hamilton and Joe Greene. John and Suzie acknowledged the people's greetings, and posed for numerous photo shots. They all finally were able to drive away.

'We want to bring you up to date on what has happened here', Joe said. 'Suzie, your mother has filed for a divorce from her husband. We talked to her attorney, and he also indicated she was very depressed about losing you. She has instructed him to tell you all of your father's estate will be turned over to you', he said.

John and Suzie rode in silence the rest of the way. John knew that Suzie was very pleased with the news the men had brought them. He squeezed her hand and got an instant reply. All her worries were melting away. It would take time, and a lot of prayers. She did not seek revenge. She wanted love, and she wanted to give love. Prayer will bring both relief and answers, were her thoughts.

CHAPTER 133

*A*n idea had begun bouncing around in John's thoughts ever since they left their plane-wreck haven. As Suzie would call it - our 'oasis'. His father, mother and sister's estates had made him quite well-off in a financial way. He wanted to pursue the possibility of buying the land on and around the crash site. He could imagine creating a resort of sorts at the location.

There was a nice stream just below where the they were marooned. A dam could be built to create a large lake for a seaplane dock, and a pier for fishing and swimming. He envisioned a large lodge, surrounded by small cabins, and recreational facilities for family vacations.

There was both a romantic and spiritual aurora associated with the place. The families of those who died there should find it comforting in having the area set aside as a memorial. He could see a small chapel located down the hill close to the site, dedicated to the loved ones still resting in eternal sleep nearby.

He would find a pastor family to live on the site, to perform services at the church. He would advertise the beauty of couples getting married, and spending their honeymoon at the place where he and Suzie would be joined in wedlock. He was dreaming, he knew, but he would talk to Suzie and find out what her thoughts were on his brain-storming ideas.

CHAPTER 134

Suzie had moved in with Grandma, as she wanted to be called. It was love at first sight for the both of the women. The young lady looked so much like her beloved Jeanie, and has so many of her mannerisms, as most teenager do, the elder woman thought.

John had arranged for a decorator firm to assist in whatever changes Suzie wanted to make in her rooms. There was an area John had when he lived there, which was a mini apartment, complete with a separate entrance and a large enclosed porch.

Suzie loved the male decor of the place, but John and Grandma Stevens talked her into making it more 'Her' place. Suzie knew that this was going to be 'Their' hang-out, if she had anything to do with it, so she settled on some changes, but left enough of John's aura to remind her of her lover. Every night as she prepared for bed, she was reminded of their moments together, and her prayers were for their future.

Suzie enrolled in the University and was truly surprised how many students and faculty knew her. It became an immediate concern for her by the attention of several aggressive males. It was going to be a delicate balance of her normal friendliness, and making it plain she was not an available female.

John had helped pick out her engagement ring, and she wore it all the time, but her beauty drew a lot of admiration. When she mentioned this to John, he suggested he would visit her in school later. He felt there had to be a reminder to one of the football players who this woman was engage to. Suzie let him know that she could handle the situation on her own, but John did call a few of his friends on the team to look out for her. 'Pass the word that they can look, but can not touch', he said.

CHAPTER 135

*J*ohn's dad had a large office at his business headquarters, and he moved into the apartment that his father used when working late. Since assuming control of the company, he made it his home. It was isolated from every day running of the operation, as he was only a figurehead, anyway. He had maintained his father's staff, and they ran the show. He met with them at least once a week to lend his support and advice, if needed. They were the guts and bolts of the company, and everyone worked smoothly together.

The reason he needed the office, was to plan for his project up north, and to have a place to stay. He spent a lot of time with Grandma and Suzie, but he did not spend the night there, so he had to have this place.

Today, he had a meeting with an architectural firm to go over his ideas. From the pictures taken at the site, he wanted them to come up with a panoramic view, complete with the area transformed into his planned picture, showing the various features in a three-dimensional layout. He wanted to have this to present to the authorities along with his request to buy the land he needed for the project.

When he got approval for his proposal, he would then send each of the families who lost loved ones for their input and acceptance. He also wanted to have this visual aid when he discussed this with Suzie. John still had the letter from the wife of the pilot who flew the crashed plane. He wanted to include his plan for the site when contacting her, but realized his delay might be considered rude by the young widow, so he sat down to read it.

Dear Mr. Stevens and Ms. Wells:

My name is Mrs. June Adamson. As you know, my husband, William was the pilot of the plane you were on. I am writing this letter to thank you for your report given to the people investigating the accident. We had been married only three weeks, and this was his first flight since our honeymoon. I don't want to burden you with my grief, I just want you to know that it is far better, knowing that Bill's actions was heroic and that you have said those actions saved your lives. I would like very much to hear from you for a personal account of my husband's last moments. We are both about your age, Mr. Stevens. Your story of survival makes it a little easier for me to bear the loss of my Bill. Please write. I need your comments very much.

CHAPTER 136

*J*ohn took the letter for Suzie to read. He knew it would make her very upset to hear such a sad story, but he knew they both had to answer this request. Every evening, after their meal with Grandma, and a couple hours of visitation, John and Suzie would retire to her rooms for their special time together. There was very little of the tension they had experienced while marooned. They prayed together before the start of the ritual they observed each time they were alone. They would hold hands, signaling each other their love, and cuddle and talk. John later handed her the letter, as they sat together.

Moments passed before Suzie was able to talk. All the emotions she had felt during their ordeal came to the surface of her thoughts. John was holding her tightly and she sobbed on his shoulder.

'Oh, John, how sad. We will each write June, and maybe that will help her. Someday, let's plan to visit her, okay?', she said.

'We will, Suzie. I am working on something right now along those lines. I'll have more to say about it in a few days. We won't forget June, or any of the others that were on our flight. Right now, I want to devote all my thoughts and actions on you, sweet woman', he said. I know you have to study. You have gone out your way to spend time with Grandma, and you have helped her so much. She acts 10 years younger, and looks 20 years younger. Maybe we can do something for June to lighten her load. You never know what affect we have on others without ever knowing it. Sometimes it is bad, but we will always try for the good things, eh, sweetheart?', he said.

They had followed their daily routine that was so enjoyable, now their parting prayer was offered up to the Lord. 'Make me an instrument of thy will, oh Lord!'

CHAPTER 137

Sam Browne was on the phone with John. 'I need your services again, Mr. Browne. I want to buy about 200 acres on and around the crash site. He explained what his plans were. 'My goodness, John, that is a wonderful idea. No one could object to such a use for the area', he said.

'Here is what I need. Start the ball rolling on the purchase. Get a survey team to the site. I need a complete topographic map sent to me asap. Contact the governor and try to get him behind us.

I'll send you everything we plan to do as soon as I get them. Put feelers out for a good general contractor', John said. 'I have a retired pastor and his wife in mind for your chapel', Sam said.

'I know you can't keep this under wraps, but let's avoid publicity until we get everything lined up. You might want to use you influence to see if you and your associates might want to explore the land around my project. If this thing gains the support and blessing that I think it will, others with less noble ideas that I envision for this will try to surround it with their brand of commercialism. They could infiltrate our 'haven', big time', John said.

'We really need a buffer zone just in case. I'll help if you can get a group together. I really want this place to be available to all decent people, and to be remembered as a place of tragedy for some, elevated to a refuge and a place of renewal for all', he said. 'I know that sounds really noble, but I have been pondering this ever since we left there, and will devote myself to the project', he added.

'I haven't spoken to Suzie about this. I want to have the visible architectural presentation to show her. It may seem weird to some for me to want a place like that when it was so tragic an event. I want to include all the families affected by the wreak, with more than just token participation', he said.

'We will look into that, John. I understand what you foresee, and even though this is not private land, there could be problems. I'll get everything to you right away', he said.

CHAPTER 138

John didn't want to write to Mrs. Adamson until he could finalize his plans for the site. He really did not know how she would react to his efforts since her husband's body was intact and not scattered all over the place, and may not want such a reminder.

'I'm working on something to insure our 'haven' will survive, Suzie. I should have something to show you in a couple days. It would be much better to have plans and pictures than to try to tell you what I want to do. It does not mean those plans should be considered anything more than just plans at this time. You will be an important source of ideas and help toward our goal for such a project. If you want to write to June, go ahead. I want present our ideas to her about the site along with visual aids. If you do write, mention that we have some ideas about the place.

Maybe we can get her feelings. She may want to shun anything about the whole idea', he said.

CHAPTER 139

June Adamson had followed the drama unfolding at the crash scene of her husband's plane. The couple that had survived left a few days before she got there to claim his body. The folks there had explained to her how the man, John Stevens, had protected the cockpit, which was almost intact, by sealing it with some metal sheet. He was afraid animals might disturb the two pilots' remains.

They gave her a copy of the report given to them by Ms. Wells and him. It described the pilot's action and was full of praise for his skill and courage. Mr. Stevens had given thanks to his devotion throughout, when he must have known they were going to crash, yet held the plane steady through the long glide.

Mr. Stevens had compared the pilots' actions with those of the plane that had been landed in the Hudson river, the only difference was that there was no river, just a dense forest. And he almost pulled off as much of, or even more of, a miracle. He didn't save all his passengers, but his final maneuver kept two of them alive.

She had given a letter to be presented to the pair on their return flight, but they had not responded. She was very anxious to hear from them, and was finally rewarded by a letter from Ms. Wells.

It was just the kind of letter she had needed. Never in her life had she felt so alone these past few days. Was it really that long since she heard the knock on her door, and saw the two men standing on the porch. It seems time has changed for her forever.

Little did she know just how much this letter from Ms. Suzie Wells would completely impact on her future. Nothing Suzie wrote was very dramatic. Mostly she wrote of what happened to her, and how the time marooned together with John changed her so much.

She said that they were in the process of insuring that the crash site be made into a permanent resort, kind of. She wanted her to comment on what her ideas might be for maintaining the area as some kind of sanctuary to the memory of those lost that day.

'Please stay in touch with us. I have two years of school ahead before John and I can get married. It seems like a long time, but we will both be busy while I grow up. That sounds funny to me right now. I have had to make some very adult decisions lately concerning my future, but mine don't feel as important when I compare them with yours. We are truly interested in all the lives who were on that plane, but you and your husband are really special. Maybe we could have a reunion at the site, or a visit to your home-town. Please consider meeting with us.

John will write later, June. He has taken over the family business, and he is working on our 'memorial'. Thank you for your letter. We both cherish it deeply', Suzie said.

CHAPTER 140

The survey had arrived yesterday, and a group were poring over the lay-out. Along with the photographic panoramic view, everyone agreed the site could become a beautiful; John didn't know how to describe the place. To Suzie and him, it would be sort of their 'haven'.

To the surviving family members of those who died there, it would be something else. And to visitors and the outside world, it would be a place to have a vacation. Right now, the architectural boys were doing most of the planning, and John liked their ideas.

'Let's allow these guys to come up with a lay-out, and we'll go over what they propose', he said. He would talk to Suzie about what they would call this- 'spot'.

John had received good enough news from Sam about acquiring the land for his project, to call the meeting he just left.

'Your plans for the crash site got rave notices from everyone. As long as they don't have to spend money, these people will approve anything to advance tourism for this area. I have business people interested in the surrounding acres, so we will proceed with that item right away', he said. 'I'll send you everything as soon as finalize plans here, Sam.

It will take a couple years to complete this project, as winter will close it down, and we are in no hurry to finish before Suzie reaches her magic birthday. You know, all of our plans center around that woman's come-of-age occasion, and I wouldn't have it any different. Lucky for us, it's in the summer. I'll bet it is a pretty place that time of year. Suzie and I only saw it in the winter, yet it is a nice scenic spot, as long as there is not a blizzard raging through the trees', John said.

CHAPTER 141

*J*ohn and Suzie had finished their dinner meal with Grandma. 'I'm sort of a tired tonight, John, so I'm going on to bed. I took a sleeping pill that has really worked on me', she said, as her caretaker led her to her quarters. John cuddled Suzie close, as they watched the local television station. A segment was announcing the start of the annual Miss Teen America pageant. Applicants for the city crown could pick up forms from the headquarters located downtown. 'Suzie, why don't you enter that contest?', John asked.

'Oh, John, you are hilarious. I love you for thinking I could compete in a beauty contest, thou. Not everyone is blinded by my looks, however', she said.

'Well, I admit my bias, young lady, which proves I have a keen eye for adorable females. This city would embrace you with open arms, because you are pretty, and they see you as I do. A remarkable human being', he said. 'Think about it, my sweetie. You are young only once, and I worry that all this happening to you might be taking away some of your youthful experiences', he said.

Suzie realized that her boyfriend/fiancé was still concerned about their relationship. And she was pleased to hear him express himself. She was in love with him, and nothing would ever change that, she thought. Yet, she knew other girls her age were engaged in activities that were denied to her. Parties, double dates, and flirting with the guys. The one thing she always reminded herself about, however, was that almost all those young ladies would gladly trade places with her. It showed in their eyes and body language when she and John were together in public. 'We all make choices in life that may turn out bad, but I am so pleased and happy being here with you', she said.

John's love and respect for her radiated from him, and she gloried in every minute of their display of devotion to one another. She realized John wanted to show her off, because he truly liked her, as well as 'love her'.

'Okay, I will pick up the form after school tomorrow. You make me feel good when you worry about me. I really am a positive thinker, John, and completely content with my life right now. We are moving forward together just as I dreamed we would', she said, as she snuggled close.

CHAPTER 142

*J*ohn arose from his bed with an extra bounce in his step. Everything was moving along so well. He had a big meeting this morning with the architects here, and a conference call with Sam.

Then he was off to watch Suzie's first audition at the pageant. All of the contestants would be there, and he was anxious to see the competition. Her entry made the front page, and was a lead story on one television program.

Everyone had heard of her, and saw her picture almost every day after they gotten back home. Just as he had predicted to her before, she was flooded with mail, and a number of marriage proposals. They both got some good laughs at some of them. Old, young, tall and short; swearing their undying love for her.

John figured it would be even worse, once the media begins their focus on this contest.

It took only a few hours watching and listening to the contestants for the on-lookers to realize who was going to get the city's beauty prize. John was indeed pleased with the poise Suzie displayed. The applause was robust after her talent presentation. She tried not to look his way, but he could tell she was happy with his reaction to her performance. And so were the judges. They would not make any decisions today, but everyone felt his beautiful fiancée would represent them in the state contest next month.

'You were so good, Suzie. I was very surprised to hear you sing', he said. 'Dad's training helped me so much. We use to practice together a lot, and I took voice lessons, at his urging. Little did I know I would be needing the training to be a beauty contestant', she laughed.

Her eyes moistened at the thought of her father, and the times they sang together in church. How heavy would her heart be, if John had not come along to ease her lose, and help fill the gap he left. She was so glad all her memories of growing up with him were good ones. 'I hope this will not be last time I do this.

There are some pretty girls I am up against out there', she said. 'This will be a cake-walk. The big test is the state prize', John said.

CHAPTER 143

'Let's go to my office. I have something to show you. I have been working on a project I know you will interested in', he said. The architectural firm had the presentation neatly detailed on a disc, with aerial shots mixed with drawings of how the whole place would look like. As John turned on the presentation, Suzie gasped as the first thing shown was their 'haven'. Tears came to her eyes as John explained what his plans were for the area, as the visual lay-out was being shown.

'I want you to help with your ideas about this project, Suzie. This place will be for us, and for all the people affected by the crash. It should be finished just about on your birthday next year, and I want you to tell me if you will marry me in this chapel, being shown right here', he said.

'Oh, John, what a wonderful plan! You can tell from my tears what I think of the whole idea, especially our wedding. I love you, dear man', she exclaimed. 'I will have a hard time waiting for that day to come. God has blessed us so much, John. We are together, I feel, because He has a plan for our lives. It will be up to us to find the way, and then to direct our lives toward His will. Maybe we can be an influence on other lives. I am thinking right now of Mrs. Adamson, John.

From her letter, she left me the impression that her family was not connected to her very strongly. She must be so lonely and in need of friends. Let's make a big effort to reach out to her', Suzie said. Since we are both so tied down here, I was thinking of inviting her to visit us', she said.

'We need to meet her first, and spend a little time together. I'm going to write, and throw out the idea of us spending a day with her in her town', Suzie said.

We can spare a Saturday and Sunday, don't you think', John asked. 'Grandma is doing so well, let's ask her to go along as our chaperon', he said.

'Ok, the first weekend for me will be after the state pageant finals next month.

That is also when I have a break in school'. Suzie said. 'That will give us time to plan the trip', John said.

CHAPTER 144

At first, the letter from John and Suzie was just a pleasant occasion in June's every day life, but that feeling quickly changed to one of overwhelming joy.

'We would like to come visit you', they wrote. 'How about us planning a week-end together in about a month. There is so much to talk over, and we do want to meet you', were their words.

Her world had been destroyed by the loss of her young husband, and she was so alone and lonesome. The revelation that someone cared about her brought her to tears. She thought there were none left in her, since so many had flowed in the past few weeks. The couple had enclosed a photo of themselves, and John's grandmother.

'We want to bring 'Grandma' with us. She will be our chaperon, but she is so much more than that to us', John wrote. 'This is something we really look forward to doing, so please let us know your thoughts', they penned.

June called the telephone number Suzie and John had sent in their letter. Suzie answered and the two had a long and enjoyable conversation. It was apparent to them both that they were going to be good friends. June remembered the references both the young people had made about their Christian faith. She had been raised in such an environment, but had not retained a lot since leaving home for school, and getting married.

Her worry was that they would be overly demonstrative and zealous in their devotion, and it might create tension she would not be comfortable with. Her fears were unfounded, as Suzie spent most of the time trying to console the young widow. They soon began planning for their meeting, and June was left with the wonderful feeling of expectation toward the visit.

'We will have completed plans for what we want to do at the crash site, June. Your ideas are needed, so think about what you might want the place to be. And don't hold back if you disagree with what is proposed. Remember, this will only be the start of the planning', Suzie said.

CHAPTER 145

*E*verything was coming together quite well on the 'Project', as the memorial was being called at John's office. All the details on the acquisition of the land and the plans were approved by all agencies involved. Sam had done his part to perfection, and John had rewarded him with a handsome monetary stipend. He and his partners had secured most of the land next to the project.

They would build a nice helicopter landing area close by, to accommodate transportation to and from the area. That, plus the lake for seaplane access, would be the only way into the place. 'That is great news.'

'As soon as we get those items completed, we can begin bringing in the construction crews and materials', John said.

Everyone was in John's office, and they were on a conference call with Sam. 'There may changes, because I want to consult with all the families involved for their views. I don't expect there will be many, but I will put a time when everything is finalized', he said, as he closed the meeting.

Suzie had sat thru the deliberations at John's request. He wanted her to hear it all, so she could call June with the news. They had the dates all set for their visit.

'I am really surprised how much we both are looking forward to our trip', Suzie said. 'All this talk and planning about our 'haven' has stirred my soul, John. Some sweet memories are coming back, and I want June to learn to love the place as we do. Maybe, right now, she can't view it as we do, but when she sees what we are going to do, all that will change. At least, I hope and pray it will. Thanks for keeping everything alive up there, sweetheart. There is very little you could do that would surpass this. Well, maybe a few things, but you know what I mean', she said.

CHAPTER 146

'We are anxious to meet June because we know how attached she is to our place, and to us. Her letter back to us, and her phone calls make it quite clear that she is looking forward, also, to seeing us', he said.

Little did they know just how intertwined their lives were to be with the life of June Adamson, in the future. Fate had brought all this about, but how it would affect them, lie in the hands of each of them individually. The way each handled themselves could be a test from God as to each of their faiths, both in the Almighty, and in their own selves. Each would face the future together, and yet alone to make choices that would affect everyone.

CHAPTER 147

*T*hings were beginning to get a little hectic in Suzie's world. Their trip to visit June had finally been finalized. Grandma was shocked at first at the invitation to be a part of the adventure, claiming her age prevented such travel, but as she had time to think about it, she realized it would good for her to get away with the kids.

Suzie's time was taken up by school, preparations for the state pageant, and getting ready for their journey. John was busy with his project, as he called it, and the month seemed to have flown by for them all.

The state event was first up, and the excitement that John and Grandma showed was contagious, and most of Suzie's reluctance was gone. The only thing she disliked was the swimsuit display. Most of the contestants wore bikini style outfits, but hers was a simple one-piece, old fashioned suit that John thought was stunning. He expressed his feelings by telling her that he had never seen a more perfect female figure. His admiration made her walk down the runway an enjoyable experience, and the confidant way she presented herself blew the judges and audience away.

Her beauty and poise won her the crown before they even got to the talent phase. Her performance in that segment just solidified it all. 'I want you to know, young man, that your vote tonight was registered on you face, and in your body-language, and it was the one that I cherish, John Stevens', she said.

'I am so proud of you, Suzie. That was a wonderful presentation tonight. Repeat it at the final pageant, and you could be the winner', he said.

CHAPTER 148

*T*he plane finally took off, headed north. The three of them settled down for the journey. Grandma was across the aisle by herself. She wanted to give John and Suzie some privacy, and John winked at her, and mouthed his 'thank you'. 'Suzie, I have something to tell you. Your mother was present when you were crowned 'Miss City'. I spotted her seated in the back, alone, and concealing herself, as best she could. It was obvious she did not want us to know she was there, so I didn't say anything. I looked real hard for her at the state affair, but I don't think she was there. I held off telling you, in case she was at both events, so we could approach her together. I saw her leave as soon as they announced the winner, and you could tell she was crying', he said.

Suzie was overwhelmed. She put her arms around John, and sobbed on his shoulder. The actions her mother had taken against her, had hurt her very much. The softened stance she later took eased her pain a lot, but the memories were still fresh in her mind. Not a day had passed without feeling the hurt of her actions. She had found the address and phone number of her apartment, where she had moved, and had been tempted several times to call her. John had advised her to hold off awhile, and let things alone.

'Your mother must start that action, Suzie. Give her the chance to adapt to her new life. It must be painful for her, losing a husband and her only child. My prayer is that she wants to have your forgiveness, but she must be the one to act first', he said.

Now, she had made that step, although small, but it was a move. The couple of lovers were seated on an airplane, hugging, and crying on each other's shoulder. Several nearby passengers were staring in disbelief, and one was reaching for the panic button, when John raised his head, and informed everyone that they had just received some very good news and could not contain their joy.

Suzie burst into laughter, and so did everyone around them, and the disturbance brought the flight attendants running. Grandma was the most relieved, as she had almost crossed the aisle, before the tension eased. John explained to her what had happened. She then joined them in hugs, kisses, and a few tears. She knew how much Suzie was hurting about her mother, and she had always felt that the woman would seek her daughter's forgiveness someday.

The remainder of the flight was one they would long remember, as Suzie's happiness was contagious. 'I'll write Mother and let her know she was seen at the pageant, and thank her for coming. I will assure her all is forgiven on my part, and see what happens. Maybe a few scars will remain, but let's hope and pray I can be a daughter again, and she can be 'Mother' once more', she said.

CHAPTER 149

John and Suzie had been recognized by the pilot when they boarded the plane, and he notified the airline personnel at the airport. No one knew why they were coming, but it was news, and they called the media. Just as they were getting ready to land, he had announced to the passengers of their presence. The head stewardess came back to talk to them, and asked the purpose of their visit.

Grandma was upset by her question and made her displeasure known to everyone. 'I didn't mean to offend you folks. We are all so glad to have you on board, and my curiosity got the better of my manners. Please forgive me', she said.

Suzie spoke up. 'We are here to meet Mrs. William Adamson, the wife of our pilot on that ill-fated flight. That man saved our lives, and we are here to see June, and tell her how much we appreciate him.

That information had been relayed to the airline people, and when they arrived, instead of only being greeted by June Adamson, the place was packed with media, airline people, and lots of onlookers, eager to see the couple that had become famous, not just by that incident, but by the fact the young lady was now a beauty queen. They were immediately introduced to Mrs. Adamson, but there was a delay before they could get through all the greeters, and interviews, to sit down together and become acquainted. June was surprised when the place became packed in front of the gate where John and Suzie were to deplane. Suddenly, a tv camera was turned on in her face, and a microphone appeared. She was about to be interviewed. People crowded around her to hear about her visitors who were on the plane coming in.

'Why wasn't this meeting announced to the public', was the first question. Luckily, for her, she was rescued by a pilot friend of hers and her late husband.

'Ease up, folks. This lady came here to meet some travelers, not to be waylaid by you guys. When she greets these people, she will choose whether she wants to talk to anyone else', he said.

Just then, a group of airline people surrounded June, and led her to a company lounge. 'We didn't expect this to happen, Mrs. Adamson. We will bring your guests in here as soon as possible', the pilot said.

Suzie rushed over to hug June, as they entered the lounge. It was evident the two young ladies were pleased with each other by the way they smiled, and looked one another over, as women were prone to do. Suzie felt that the young lady was still in mourning, and gave her an extra - long embrace. John and Grandma joined them, and the four began the process of becoming acquainted.

June had not expected the greeting she received from the young lady. Her reaction was one of relief and joy, however, as it was a warm and genuine embrace between them. She acknowledged the others, and was impressed with both their appearances. She could see how Suzie had fallen in love with this handsome man. A sad expression fell across her face, as she recalled how much in love she was with her husband. Suzie sensed her feelings and said, 'I'm sorry'.

Their eyes met, and both teared up, as they hugged. Grandma came over and joined them.

John knew that this was a 'woman' moment, and walked out of the lounge. He needed to talk business with the airline, and this was the time to do it, leaving the ladies to strengthen their bonding.

As they talked, no one would have guessed that just a few months ago, each were completely unknown to the other. Maybe there was some truth to the phrase: 'familiarity leads to contempt'. With no background issues or history between them, they were free to become genuine friends, almost from the very beginning. They were starting a relationship that would last the rest of their lives, and would affect the course of John Stevens' future. Indeed, the future of them all in a profound way.

CHAPTER 150

*J*ohn and Suzie had not envisioned the wonderful rapport developing with June Adamson. It was apparent, after the planned two-day visit, everyone was eager to extend their stay. all of the time spent together, had been in the suite at the hotel, even their meals. The reason was the relentless media request on them all. It was a blessing in disguise as the time was well spent. John secured the adjoining room for June, so she did not have to go home. John had the room on the other side, and the meetings between them all were in the large living room. The three women included John most of the time, but it was evident that Suzie and June were becoming fast friends.

'I feel like she is the sister I always wanted, and even prayed for', she confided in John. 'Have you noticed the change in her, John. When we first met her, the tension in everything she did was so plain to see. Now, she laughs a lot, and she is relaxed around us. We really are lucky the media forced us to become friends. How ironic', she said.

'Yes, we have made a difference in her, for sure. And this has made as much a change in us', John said. You have needed a young woman-friend, Suzie. The lack of motherly affection and attention must be hard on you, sweetheart. Let's see if June would like for us to extend our visit a day or so', he said. The airline people want us all to be their guests at a memorial dinner for everyone lost in the crash tonight. I haven't mentioned this to June, because she seemed to become emotional in a hurry when she is reminded of her husband. Come on, we can talk to her now', he said.

Grandma was telling June about her late husband, and the additional loss of the others so soon afterwards, had been so difficult to bear. June realized that this kind woman had suffered, as she had. It made it a little easier to remember. John and Suzie came into the room and sat down with them.

'We have been invited to a memorial dinner tonight, June. The airline is honoring those that were lost on the plane. I know you will not want to be reminded, and I am reluctant to bring it to your attention', he said. June stood, and turned to face them. 'Two days ago, I would have never gone to such a meeting. But, here comes you people, with your love and understanding, changing me from a self-pity widow, to back to whom I really am. I'm really will never be the person I once was, and I don't want to be. I will gladly go, but we women have to do some shopping, am I right, ladies? Everyone broke down laughing at the sudden change in the room. 'Yes, we do', Grandma said. 'One more thing before you leave me high and dry' John said. We want to stay a couple days longer, if everyone agrees', OK?

CHAPTER 151

*T*he letter in her box was addressed to Mrs. Barbara Sloan. After her divorce, Suzie's mother had reverted to her previous husband's name, so it was a mild shock to receive a letter from someone using her old name. It became a really huge shock when she saw who it was from. Her daughter had written to her, and she could hardly read it through the tears. She had been seen at the pageant by the girl's fiancé, and Suzie thanked her for coming, and expressed her hope they could get together someday soon.

It was not an unfriendly note, but there was a subdued theme in her daughter's words. Barbara accepted this as a first step being made to reach out, to returned the mother's overture. She deeply rued her actions toward Suzie. Maybe the mother-daughter bond was strong enough to overcome the wrong she had done. Probably not totally, but this little bit made her very happy. Suzie had included her address, so Barbara felt she wanted to hear from her. She vowed to do everything she could to make up for her past actions. 'I love you, dear daughter. I will make you believe I am indeed sorry for hurting you', she whispered.

The visit was coming to an end, and everyone was unhappy to part company. 'We had such an enjoyable time with you, June. It is so good that you have agreed to come to the opening of our 'Journey's End', Suzie said.

John has purposed the name for their project at the crash site, but they were going to ask for others to come up with a title. 'I know it is over a year away, but we are looking forward to meeting everyone associated with the event. In the meantime, we want you to consider visiting us at home as soon as possible.', John said.

The three women had become close in the few days since they met, especially June and Suzie. There were tears and hugs all around as they prepared to board the plane. June was so much more 'alive', John noted, and they both were so pretty. Everyone kept looking their way, and all the airline people were there to see them off, as well as the media. Word had gotten out about the project, and there were a lot of questions being asked. 'There will be an announcement coming out as soon as we have it all put together, so be patient', John told the reporters.

John and Suzie, from the first day they got home, had made sure there was plenty of their 'close' time together. All the outside activities that took so much of the day just increased the intensity of being in love. They both knew everything pointed to the moment they were married. 'I focus so much on that event, that I need to remind myself of the fact this be only the beginning for us', Suzie said.

They had both read the letter Suzie had waiting for her when they returned home from their trip. It was a nice message from her mother, but Suzie was reminded of the pain she had endured. 'All of that is in the past and is forgiven, but the hard part is to forget', Suzie said. 'I'm learning, thou. Mother seems sincere and I am going to do my share to put it all to rest'.

The next several months seemed to literally fly by for everyone since their visit. Suzie had to balance school work against pageant demands. She had called her mother and the two began the slow process of regaining trust in each other. She talked to June several times a week and the young widow expressed her desire to attend the state pageant event, which was coming up. 'You will come straight to our house, and we will drive together. It's only a one-hour trip, which Grandma and I will use to catch up on what you have been doing', Suzie said.

CHAPTER 152

The project up north was developing really fast. 'I am going to come visit as soon as the state contest is over, Sam', John said. 'It is hard to believe almost a year has passed since they left the wreak area. Your estimate about finishing seems to be right on. I'll fill you in as to our plans on when we will open up. It all depends on Suzie's results next week. If she wins, that will add some time before we make any further decisions right now', he said. 'Well, everyone is pulling for her up here.

This whole area has turned into a really huge cheering section for you guys. Not a day goes by I don't get a dozen or more inquiries about when they will see you folks again', Sam said.

The time was fast approaching when John and Suzie were going to have to decide on a date for their wedding. The place was settled. Their wonderful event would open, 'The haven of Rest'.

'John, I want our life together to be our 'lives' beginning. I have been keeping a record this past year, of my days during each month when I can get pregnant. I want us to start your and our 'lives' together on our honeymoon where we fell in love. The day of the month is set by my biological clock, John. Oh, I can see by your eyes and that grin, you like the idea', she exclaimed, as she rushed into his arms. 'Now let's get this pageant thing behind us, and we will be ready to go', Suzie said.

They arrived at the auditorium. Suzie, June and Grandma went back stage to prepare for the event. John was staying out of sight, as he suspected Suzie's mother would be coming, and he wanted to meet her and bring her to their reserved seats. Since she was family, they would all sit together.

John knew that would please everyone. The media would probably make a big deal of it all, so he approached the head guy in charge of the station from their home town, to alert him of what John thought would happen. 'Please don't overdo this angle', he said. The reporter was aware of the events between daughter and mother, so agreed to keep everything low-key.

At that moment, Mrs. Sloan walked into the hall. John recognized her and approached her immediately. 'I am John Stevens, and I am so glad to meet you', he said.

The lady took a step backwards, as the encounter took her completely by surprise. The shock of meeting this young man was amplified by the television camera recording the whole thing. The station crew had immediately sprung into action, as soon as they realized what was happening. Her first reaction was to flee, but John smiled broadly, took her arms, and directed her to their seats.

'Don't let the media upset you, Mrs. Sloan. They see a story developing, but we are not going oblige them, are we'?, John exclaimed. Suzie will be thrilled that you are here, so will my grandmother, and the other person in our party, June Williams. She is the widow of the pilot of our plane. We have become good friends with her, and you will like her. Now, as for me, I want to assure you, I am totally in favor of your efforts to reconcile with Suzie. We both want you back in her life, and I thank you for making this all possible', he said.

Barbara Wells followed John to the reserve section where they were seated. Her anxiety had subsided as John's manner helped so much to put her at ease. But the tension she felt was about her daughter. How would she react to seeing her next to the young woman's fiancé?

CHAPTER 153

*T*he contestants came on stage and were introduced to the world. Suzie immediately spotted her mother, and all her nervousness disappeared. She could not resist waving to her. Everyone's attention was drawn to the gesture for a few seconds, as Barbara beamed at her daughter. The pageant proceeded along and it came time to announce the winners.

Suzie was alone at the end with one other contestant. It would be one of the two crowned the winner. Suzie was introduced as the runner-up, and she burst into tears. She congratulated the young lady, and said-'thank you', and walked toward where her family was seated. She was asked to stop and talk to a reporter.

'You must deeply disappointed', the man said, as Suzie was still softly crying. 'No, I am not shedding tears of sorrow. I am overjoyed at being named the runner-up. It is an honor I will always cherish, but this means the end to the only thing keeping me from my marriage to John Stevens. We can know set the date, and it will be real soon', she beamed.

She ran to where John was waiting for her, and the whole world knew how she felt about where her future was headed. She brought her mother, June and Grandma into their embrace, and it turned into a bawling, happy display of human love. They had captured the spotlight, and Suzie was going to make the most of it.

'John, I want to announce right now, on this state-wide program, our wedding date. Three weeks from today will be 22nd of the month. Will you marry me on that day'?, she asked. They all squealed at the same time, drawing the camera crew being drawn closer by their outburst.

'We want to make an announcement. John and I will be married on the 22nd of this month at our 'Haven of Rest', the site of the plane crash where we fell in love. I want to ask June Adamson, widow of our pilot on that flight, to be my maid-of-honor. June, please do me the honor, and say, yes', she pleaded.

CHAPTER 154

*T*he ride home was filled with laughter and rejoicing. They had all gather around Suzie and her mother as Barbara was leaving by herself. 'I would ride with you, Mom, but I can't leave John now', she said.

'Don't worry about that, Suzie. I am more than fine at this time. I came real close to remaining at home, so I have a lot to be thankful for this trip. We'll get together in a couple days. I want to spend some time with you guys', she said.

'June, will you stay here with us, and we can all go together for the wedding'?, Suzie asked.

'That's fine. We have a lot to do in a hurry. I can't believe how quickly everything got turned around. One minute, we are praying for a beauty queen award, the next thing I know, I'm to be a brides-maid. You know, I was feeling so sorry for you, and then we find out you never wanted to win', June said.

The two young ladies were joined in hilarious laughter by Grandma, as they sat having lunch. June felt all her past depression steadily going away, and being replaced with a wonderful will to live. 'We are going to have to do a lot of shopping tomorrow', Suzie said.

'I am looking forward to it', June answered. She was looking ahead, past the wedding, and knew the future beckoned her. Little did she know just how that future was going to be tied to this beautiful family.

CHAPTER 155

*J*ohn chartered a Learjet to transport the wedding party. They couldn't land at the resort, so flew in on three seaplanes from the nearest airport. Professor Hamilton came along. He was to be John's best man. Then, there were four bridesmaids, Suzie's mother, Grandma, June, and the bridal couple. They came several days early, to enjoy the new facilities. It was in the late summer, and the weather was perfect. Several families of victims of the wreak had taken John up on his invitations to visit the area, and to attend the wedding.

There were cabins dotted around the central lodge, and the chapel. The crash zone was preserved as a memorial section, with a bench beside a stand with the name of individuals inscribed. Each cabin bore one the names, also, and were reserved for the family one week of the year.

Up the hill, dominating the heights, was the tail section of the plane, nested between the two trees, where it saved the lives of John and Suzie. Everyone made a tour of their 'haven', and it was obvious they all were happy with what had been done to the area all around it, with flower beds dotting the landscape, and gravel paths connecting everything. It was a place with sadness for some, and joy for others, but it would soon be a beautiful and serene location attracting couples and families from around the world.

Among the families of the crash victims was a lone man. Jack Marson, jr. was the only child of Jack and Freida, who were aboard the fateful flight. The young doctor had finished medical training and wanted to meet John. He introduced himself, and immediately asked a favor.

I love the nice cabin you have named for my parents. I would like to build a medical clinic in their names, and start my career here. I am doing research work and want to use this place as my base. Modern communications allows me to connect to the world from most anywhere. This is my choice, if you agree', he said. 'I will have plenty of time to devote the clinic to people visiting or to permanent residents. I want to be near my parents and I would like to donate the clinic in their names', he said.

'Could you use a certified RN at such a place? John asked. 'Yes sir. Do you have anyone in mind?, Jack replied.

'I might have. We'll inquire and keep you posted', John said.

The network that had landed first and recorded their meeting with John and Suzie, had contacted them as soon as news came out about the opening of the resort, and the wedding. 'We want to bring in a crew and record the event', the CEO said. 'That includes your wedding, if we may. We will not be intrusive at all, I promise, and I assure you that our people will respect the area for what it is. To you and all the others there', he said.

'OK, but you can only stay the day of the wedding. That will give you ample time to take everything in. I don't want any hint of commercialism, or carnival atmosphere portrayed. I want it recorded, so I can review it before airing, if you please', John said.

John escorted June toward a young man standing alone by the Chapel. 'June, I want you to meet Dr. Jack Marson, jr. He is going to build a clinic right next to this building. His parents were aboard our ill-fated plane, June. He will dedicate the structure to them, he said.

There was an immediate bond between the young couple, and it was two-fold. First, the shared grief of losing so much at this site, as they shook hands. It was coupled with the fact neither looked upon this place in a morbid way. Their loved ones were here, so it was a good place.

Second, June was a RN and they connected due to the medical background they shared.

John sensed the attraction, and said a prayer, asking the Lord to please help these young folks find something together in their lives, both profession and personal.

He excused himself, leaving their presence.

The time of the wedding had arrived. Everything went letter perfect. It was a solemn crowd that had sat quietly through the ceremony, and the newly-weds exit from the church, but erupted into applause and celebration as everyone gathered in the lodge's ballroom, for joyous feasting and dancing. They had planned events, so that twilight would be upon them a couple hours after the wedding.

As dusk arrived, John and Suzie, separately went among the guests, greeting each one warmly. 'I want to ask everyone to join Suzie and me in a pray, if you will', John said. Afterwards, they said their farewells, joined hands, and began the walk up the hill to their 'haven'. They paused at the door. John took his bride up into his arms, and they crossed the threshold together. There was not a dry eye in the crowd, as everyone was overwhelmed by the occasion. No one could ever forget this moment, and the recording crew was making sure it would be available to the world.

CHAPTER 156

'John, I have news for you', Suzie said as she greeted her husband of three weeks.

John acted normally, not revealing his "guess', as to the news coming up. He had kept up with the calendar, and knew Suzie was overdue for her period. He made no mention of it, when his bride had told him she had an appointment with the doctor today. It was the hardest thing he had gone through in his life, not to shout his feeling to the world this morning, for he was sure he was going to be a father. He remained calm, as Suzie began her solemn announcement—she was pregnant.

Then, he exploded in the joy of the news. Grandma came running as best she could, at the outburst. It scared her and the caretaker nurse with her, and both were visibly relieved to see the grins on the young couple's faces.

There were hugs and kisses all around, as everyone knew Suzie had been anxiously waiting for this event. The newly-weds were ready to raise a family. 'I've got to call mom, and June', she said. She talked every day with each of them, so they knew about the appointment.

Suzie was trying very hard to restore completely, the relationship with her mother, and it was slowly coming around. There was no such feeling when it came to June, though. Suzie missed her new-found friend very much. It was mutual between them, and they were on the phone for long periods of time.

June had gone home after the wedding. John and Suzie had begged her to go back with them, but she felt she would be over staying her welcome, if she did. Their time together had really helped the young widow regain some of her zest for life. The trip to the crash site had set her back, though. Only until the end did she finally overcome the negative side of the place. At the end, she truly fell in love with everything about it. Her last moments on 'their bench', as she called the spot, were serene and sweet. The memory of her husband, William, was not exactly fading, but was slowly slipping peacefully into her past. There was still that one regret gnawing at her soul.

They had made the decision to put off having a family. 'We will have plenty of time later', June told her new husband. Not a day has passed since his death, has she forgotten that. It was brought back so forcibly as she sat watching John and Suzie enter their haven. The two women had talked the day before, and Suzie told June of her plans to start her family.

'I wish every day that Bill and I had done that', she said. Now, she needed to get on with the 'now and the future', of her life. Her friendship with Suzie and John, and Grandma did make it worthwhile living, and they were so regular with their calls, and letters. She had never written anyone before, so she was not prepared for the joy and excitement she got out of hearing from them. She realized how different it was from a phone call. It was nice talking, but it could be described as being warm and personal when it came to the letters.

There was a new development in her life, however. Dr. Jack Marson had entered very subtly into her future. He had asked her to join in his clinic work and research at the crash site, when June revealed her profession.

'I need an assistant, June. Will you consider working with me? This place is going to be my office, and my home for a long time, because of my parents', he said

The thought of moving forward in her life was drawing her toward accepting the doctor's offer. She could not remain in mourning forever, she thought.

CHAPTER 157

Suzie's call and announcement made June's day, for sure. The two talked for quite some time, catching up with each other, as if they were sisters. Suzie mentioned this and they both realized that both felt the same way about that. 'Oh, June, we want to come visit you real soon. Please invite us, will you? We can come any time', she said.

'That would be wonderful, Suzie. I want you to know, however, I may be going to work for Dr. Marson at his clinic. I'm sure John has mentioned the possibility to you. I'll let you know when I decide', she said.

Fate stepped in, shortly thereafter, in the lives of John and Suzie. 'The spotting you experienced last night, Suzie, is an indication you are going to have to stay off your feet for a couple days', the doctor declared. 'There is nothing serious that I can see, but let's be cautious. We will do some blood tests, to try to find the cause, in the meantime', he said.

'That eliminates our trip to see June', Suzie said. 'John, can we invite June to come here? I don't know if she will, but I really want to spend time with her', she said. 'You bet, young lady. Give her a call later. Right now, I want you to rest. The pill you just took should put you under for a-while, so turn that mind off and rest, please', he said.

CHAPTER 158

*J*une had not been happy, since returning home, if she could call it that. The apartment depressed her. She vowed to make up her mind very soon. Too many memories here, she thought. Her attitude changed immediately after receiving Suzie's call, however. 'I would love to come visit. This place is so drab after being with you guys. You take it easy, and I'll be there soon to help take care of you', she said.

June called Jack. 'Doctor Marson, I was all set to take you up on your job offer, but Suzie and John have a problem with her pregnancy, and I will be visiting them.

Please hold the invitation open. I have decided to come work with you', she said. 'Keep me posted about Mrs. Stevens, June. Most of my research has to do with human reproduction. I will welcome your being a partner in our work. Maybe we can be of help to the lady', he said

CHAPTER 159

*J*ohn was worried. Suzie and their baby were his whole world right now. He had never felt such emotions before. Suzie made him feel so good about himself. He enjoyed the close physical and spiritual relationship they had together. He realized every day how much the death of his family had affected his life, now that Suzie's love dominated him. He tried not to show his worries and concerns, but it was evident to both Grandma and his bride. 'We are going to be fine, John', Suzie said. 'The doctor will be honest and let us know if matters get worse. I should have cut back before this happened, but I couldn't seem to get enough of our wonderful life together, my sweet husband', she murmured. They always ended their day in a joint prayer, and tonight had an additional plea from the couple; to watch over them and their unborn love-child.

CHAPTER 160

*J*une's presence was felt at once. Suzie had missed her new friend, and the two spent a lot of time together. The regimen ordered by the doctor had worked, and Suzie had no more problems with the pregnancy, other than being a little weak. 'Don't worry. that can happen often during a woman's first child-bearing experience', June said. 'Do you think it will alright if I go to church this Sunday', Suzie asked the doctor.

'Sure, just don't overdo it, and stay up afterwards. I'll visit again in a couple days. I want to check the position of the fetus. I can't put a title to the little one, because you two have decided not to explore the gender of your baby. Since you are beginning your last trimester, I want to see you more often, Suzie. You are my number one concern, but not my big worry. Doctors do have favorites, in spite of the rules that discourage it', he said.

CHAPTER 161

*T*he pastor was finishing his sermon, and was inviting an altar call. Grandma and June were seated with John and Suzie, when a lady from across the church approached the front where the preacher stood. Suzie gasped, as she recognized her mother. Oh, John, our prayers are being answered. Mother is coming forward.

Let's hurry and join her', she cried. There was an emotional and heart-warming moment, when mother and daughter embraced. Most of those who witnessed this knew the history of the two women, so the reaction was overwhelming to most, but none more so than how it was affecting June.

The faith that was shown by the Steven family, including Grandma, had impressed the young widow from the beginning. She was not a stranger to religion. Her mother and father attended church, but they didn't show the same fervor, or conviction towards the tenets of Christianity. She considered herself as a believer, although she had never publicly expressed it as was now being done by Mrs. Wells. But, as she watched and listened, the need arose in her to join her loved-ones and accept Christ as her savior.

Suzie saw June approach, and was not sure why this was happening. Her prayer that the young widow would join her mother was answered, as June went toward the minister, and announced her profession. Now the praise and joy overcame Suzie, as she embraced her friend, now a sister in Christ.

CHAPTER 162

By the middle of the next day, it was evident the events at the church and the celebration later, had taken a toil on Suzie. The doctor ordered her admitted to the hospital, as she began suffering pain and cramps. The feeling of euphoria was being replaced with anxiety and apprehension.

'I can't prescribe pain pills right now due to the baby's stress', he announced.

'It is fine. I can stand the discomfort. My child's welfare comes first', Suzie said, while holding her hands with John and her mother. They limited visitors to only two, so everyone else sat waiting for news. John and Mrs. Wells came out together, and the grim look on their faces were foreboding. 'They have taken Suzie to surgery. An emergency has arisen. The baby is in danger, and will have to be taken', John cried. 'A cesarean section is happening now.

Let's join in a prayer for both of them', Susie's mother said.

The doctor stood at the door, as the family prayed. His heart was heavy at the news he must present to them. John arose, and was the first to see the man, and his whole body seemed to collapse, as he saw the expression on his face. He knew bad news was coming. The others turned to face him and they began weeping. 'Suzie is in danger. There were complications. We saved the baby, and it is a healthy, but premature girl. It will be touch and go for a few days, but your wife is a strong young lady with a will to live', he said.

CHAPTER 163

*J*ohn sat beside the hospital bed, holding his tiny daughter. 'She is indeed your baby, Suzie. Beautiful young lady', he said. There seemed to be a flicker, a slight movement from the motionless young mother and wife.

He was in his favorite place, caressing little Janice, and talking to the patient everyone was praying for.

'We have good news today, dear. Your blood pressure has been stabilized, and all tests show much improvement. Plus, the doctors plan to bring you out of the induced coma they have had you under, since Janice was born', he said.

Again, John saw a reaction from his wife. 'I feel you are aware of us, darling. Take it easy. Janice is doing great, even though she is a little premature. I get to hold her a few minutes and so will you very soon', John said.

The nurse came in as a reminder the baby had to be back in her crib. 'She is doing quite well so far. Let's not overdo it, Mr. Stevens', she said.

'I want to hold her next to her mother. Suzie seems to react to her presence', he said, as he settled the baby snug against the young mother's side.

'Did you see the eye flicker? Oh, we are all so nervous, honey. We can't wait to see your pretty smile. Janice has to go now. I hope you can hold out until tomorrow. She needs to feel her mother's heartbeat again', he said.

CHAPTER 164

Suzie's recovery was not progressing very well. She was out of immediate danger, yet she could not regain her strength. June had called Jack and mentioned Suzie's condition. 'The people here cannot pin point her problem, and I am worried', she said.

'I am going to call John and ask for Suzie's medical records. There is a group out west who is deep into conditions similar to her symptoms.

Thanks for calling, June. I hope to see you real soon', Doctor Marson said.

John and June sat around Suzie's bed, as she held Janice. The baby was doing much better than the mother, and everyone was anxious about the lingering condition of the young lady.

'Dr. Marson called, Suzie. I had the doctors here send him your charts. He had requested them. Seems there is a research team working on the very problems you are experiencing. He wants to come down and examine you. He feels certain he has the answers for your condition', John said.

'John, can we get my doctor to visit me, right away? Before we go any further, I want to talk to him', she said.

The doctor was located and asked to come to Suzie's room. 'Are you having troubles, Mrs. Stevens', he asked.

'John will fill you in on a matter, later. Right now, I want to know if I am fit to take an airplane trip of about three hours', she said.

'Well, It depends on the urgency of the trip. For a casual journey, I would say-no. Could you tell me why?', he said.

John told him of Dr. Marson and his research, and where his clinic was located.

Suzie spoke up. 'I want to go there, Doctor, for a number of reasons. I need to have the place around me. I am homesick for John's and my first dwelling. If I can be treated there, allow me to go', she asked.

'I have read of the work being done by the group you mentioned. I see no reason to object to them treating you, Mrs. Stevens', the Doctor said.

CHAPTER 165

Suzie's enthusiasm for returning to her 'home', spread to each of those who had been asked to accompany her and John. Their main concerns still centered on the young mother's health, and little Janice, but Dr. Marson was so sure he had the answer to the woman's problems.

'I can't believe all this is happening', June said. 'The hand of the Lord is directing us, for sure. Here I was dreading leaving, but so anxious to join the doctor in his work. Now, we are going to be together', she cried.

There was no hesitation on the part of John's grandmother. Her heart was set on being with what was left of her family. She loved holding the baby, and they really bonded, much to everyone's delight.

It was a different story with Suzie's mother. She wanted to go, but ever present in her mind, were reminders of past actions. June came to the rescue, as she sensed the conflict.

'You must trust the Lord, Mrs. Sloan. We have been forgiven of ours sins, by everyone. Suzie needs you, and so does your grandbaby. The love you have for them shines through, and they love you. Suzie really needs you. Not only to help with Janice, but emotionally. A daughter's love and ties never abate. You know, she was worried you would not forgive her', June said.

CHAPTER 166

*J*ohn was not aware of Suzie's desire to go back to the Park, as it is now called by nearly everyone. She had only come out of the coma a couple days ago, and the concerns about Janice and the lingering weakness of the mother, occupied their thoughts.

'I am thrilled you want to visit our place, Suzie. This is the perfect time of the year. The summer is almost gone, and the leaves will be changing soon. We haven't been there to see such a beautiful sight. Plus, Dr. Marson seems so confident he knows what is holding you back', John said.

'John, what I really want is to live there, all year round. Now, hear me out, darling. While I was lying in the hospital, unable to move, my mind kept going back to our moments together. We shared some really frightful events which I feel has shaped our future. I want to spend at least a year there, okay?', she said.

CHAPTER 167

*E*veryone settled into the new routine after the plane trip. The welcome they received was wonderful. The condition of the young mother had been a news item at home, and had spread to this area. Several camera crews were there to greet them. Dr. Marson had already been interviewed, as word had gotten out concerning the treatment he had proposed for Suzie.

'I must let the family announce any plans for Mrs. Stevens. She is still in danger, so take it easy, folks. My work here is mostly research, but the clinic is a full-fledged hospital. June Adamson is a certified RN, and will be in charge of the small staff here. We plan to stay through the winter, making it a year-round medical accommodation. I want to thank Mr. and Mrs. Stevens for giving me this opportunity to live in this place, where my parents are buried. I feel only joy and contentment as I walk along the paths. We are truly together here', he said.

CHAPTER 168

*A*long with the steady improvement of Suzie's health, there was ample evidence of another story developing in the relatively small community in the midst of the towering mountains, and multicolored leaves as fall weather had arrived. The young mother had required round the clock nursing care which meant June and Jack were working side by side most of the day. John and the other family members were there to relieve them, but sleep and rest left very little time for socializing between the couple. June welcomed the hours staying busy at the work she knew so well, and her relationship with the doctor was excellent, up to a point.

June had resigned herself to a life alone. The memories of her husband had been slowly receding in her thoughts, and becoming much more bearable. Her walks along the path to his graveside were fewer and less intense. She felt sad only just before falling asleep at night. Her feelings were more for her longing to be a mother. Janice helped, as the little girl had stolen her heart, yet it could not replace the yearning in her very being.

Everyone else in the compound, except June, could see the way Jack Marson looked at her, however. It was a respectful, subdued expression of a young man in love. His ambition to be a doctor kept him busy for the many years he studied and worked at his profession, leaving no time for a regular youthful desire for a girlfriend. Now, working alongside him was this gorgeous female whom he felt was unattainable. This fact made her even more attractive to him, and soon he had to admit, to himself, his love for her.

'June, have you thought of what you are you going to do about the doctor?', Suzie asked. 'What are talking about, Suzie?', she said.

It was a good thing June was not holding Janice, when Suzie brought to her attention the feelings the man had for her. Jack was not an unattractive young man, and June acknowledged the fact, but never considered for a moment, any thought he was 'in love', as Suzie suggested.

Suzie immediately realized her mistake. The look of shock on June's face was evidence this was news to her. The young mother began to cry, as she was filled with remorse. 'I assumed you were aware of his feeling, June. He has not spoken to anyone I know of, but It sure looks like he cares a whole lot about you', she said.

CHAPTER 169

As if on cue, Dr. Jack Marson walked into the room. He stopped dead in his tracks, on seeing his patient in tears. 'What is wrong, Mrs. Stevens?', he asked.

The two women stared at the doctor. One with tears, the other with a solemn look. June blinked, and burst into laughter. Her uproar was contagious. Suzie joined in, as they both came unglued.

Jack stood by the door, unable to fathom the cause of such behavior from these grown women. Suddenly, June looked straight into his eyes. A somber expression crossed her countenance. The woman was really, for the first time, paying attention to the appearance of this young man.

A whole new world of emotions was cruising through June's mind and body. She had buried her love and dreams and desires with the man up on the side of the hill. Not forgotten, but the loss a little bit more acceptable each day. Part of the loss, she knew, would never become easier. Her role as a wife, and her craving for motherhood would always dominate her thoughts. Now, standing in front of her was a handsome young man who was supposedly in love with her. She decided right then to do something about the rumor. Prove it true or false.

'Thanks, Suzie. I'll let you know shortly whether I will be beholden to, or hate you', she said, as she grabbed the doctor's arm and escorted him out of the room.

CHAPTER 170

*J*ack Marson was on cloud nine. Walking toward him down the Chapel aisle, escorted by her father, June was approaching him. Seated in the first row was Suzie and John, and little Janice. The treatments had brought all the youthful vigor and beauty back into the young mother's life. The doctor could not contain his happiness, as tears formed in his eyes. June noticed as she stood beside him.

'Tears of joy, my love. And for our future together', he said.

CPSIA information can be obtained
at www.ICGtesting.com
Printed in the USA
JSHW051942280322
24271JS00003BA/139